The Sea Of Clouds

To Alvina —
Hope you enjoy this coming of age tale from long ago.
Good to see you in FL,
Best,
John

Published by Global Book Publisher
Additional copies available through:
retail: www.BookSurge.com
wholesale: www.globalbookpeddler.com
Telephone: 866-308-6235 ext 20
email orders @booksurge.com

Copyright © 2003 John von Hartz
All rights reserved.
ISBN: 1-59109-948-X

The Sea Of Clouds

A NOVEL

John von Hartz

2003

The Sea Of Clouds

For Mel

THE SEA OF CLOUDS

Chapter One

It turned out to be a great day. The cool rain let up by midmorning and the skies cleared enough for our regular lunchtime game. I actually got a hit, a rarity for me, a single that barely eluded the reach of Otto Minkus and had driven in the go-ahead run. What's more, a line drive in the bottom of the inning somehow found its way into my outstretched glove, ending the game. I flopped onto the lawn in front of the turreted school building, the sun unexpectedly warm for April, a month that in Chicago is usually considered part of winter. The grass held a rich, comforting poultice on my back, a damp harbinger of a fresh growing season.

"Douglas!" The bark was familiar, the echo of a Nazi interrogation officer from movies about the recently ended war. Mike Straus stood over me, a sadistic smirk playing on his lips. "Zee Kommandant vishes your presence."

"Zee Kommandant?" This was a departure from our usual routine, which involved code words and misleading sentences to trick a spy into revealing himself and the position of the Fifth Armored Division. "Kommandant Brown, uh, Braun?"

"Jawohl. Kommandant Braun." Mike clapped his hands together sharply. "Quickly! Or must I be more *persuasive*?"

The others on the lawn began to moan. "You're up the creek," Billy Curtis sang as he slapped me with his glove. "Brown knows about you stealing the algebra exam. Joliet for life with Roger Tough Touhy as your cellmate."

"He knows what you did with Joy last Saturday night."

Otto Minkus' voice bore such conviction that a suspicion struck deep within me that he was right.

"Vy do you delay?" Mike asked. "Must I employ force?"

"I ain't saying a word without my mouthpiece," I assured those on the lawn. As if to punctuate my resolve, the bell rang, summoning us back to class. "What the hell could Dr. Brown want with me?"

"Tell me." Mike assumed the squinty-eyed mask of our customary routine. "Vere is der Fifth Armored Division?"

I tightened my expression. I wouldn't break under interrogation. I had seen enough war movies to steel me against any sneaky tactics.

Dr. Brown lurked in his garret office in the old building, which resembled a medieval castle with a huge fireplace in the baronial front hall. It lacked only a moat and guards in mailed armor brandishing pikes at the gates. He attempted to project the image of might, yet he didn't quite succeed. The problem was his looks. Assuming the role of an Oxford don, he wore heavy tweed year-round. But his gleaming pate was bottomed with a ridiculous fringe of curly white hair that flopped over his ears like a clown's fright wig. His severe metal-rimmed glasses, meant to convey the stern authority of a combat officer, couldn't bank the odd twinkle of mischievous eyes. These incongruities lent him the air of a court jester rather than a wise and feared administrator.

I tapped on the open door, readying my defense. Yes, algebra gave me fits because I didn't understand all those stupid little symbols. But I would never steal an exam. The fact that I had scored a 68 was proof enough. As for Joy last Saturday ...

"Ah, Hank Douglas. Come in. Come in."

I stood awkwardly in front of his desk.

"Sit down, please. My goodness. Yes, indeed. You should be seated when you hear what I have to say."

THE SEA OF CLOUDS

I edged into a chair awaiting the hammer blow. That was ninth grade, one body punch after another, assaults from quarters never perceived. Getting a rare hit had made my day. Now the principal urged me to sit or be knocked to my knees by his news.

"How does a year in Switzerland sound?" Dr. Brown bubbled. "On full scholarship."

"Why me?" I asked, still in my defensive stance.

"Mr. Ellis at our faculty meeting said, 'What about Hank Douglas?' We looked at one another and said, 'Why not Hank Douglas? Good student. Socially well adjusted. Team player.' It was an obvious choice. I've already spoken to your parents. We all agree it should be your decision."

"What's to decide? I'm going to Switzerland. Wherever that is."

Dr. Brown winced, unsure whether this was humor or ignorance. A splinter of doubt spiked his response. "Allow me to review the details," he hurried on. "Do you remember Josh Brackbirn?" The name meant nothing to me, as difficult as that is to imagine today. "He came here to school as a refugee from London during the war. Very intelligent. Well, you were in our elementary school then. You wouldn't have had much commerce with a high school student. Be that as it may, after some time at the University of Chicago, he returned to Europe. Now he and his mother are starting a school in Switzerland in Chaumont-sur-Neuchâtel."

The injection of French into the April air of Illinois in 1947 added to the intoxicating romantic spirit of the proposed voyage. "In appreciation for the shelter and hospitality given the Brackbirns during that trying time, they are offering a full scholarship to a student from Hillard School. They hope this will become a tradition, with a scholar from Hillard traveling to Switzerland every year on scholarship. A scholarship they have generously blessed with my name: the Gordon Brown Scholarship to the Swiss English Academy. Rather impressive, if I do say so." Dr. Brown paused to savor the moment, glancing at me over his spectacles to be sure the import registered. "You, Mr. Hank Douglas, are the first recipient of the Gordon Brown scholarship."

"Chaumont sure Neuchâtel."

"*Sur*," Dr. Brown corrected. Again a flicker of doubt flashed in his bright eyes. "Are you enrolled in a French class?"

"Latin. French is next year."

"Latin, of course. Well, with mastery of the Romance mother tongue French should pose no problem for you."

I agreed. French had to be easier than Latin, which made as much sense to me as algebra. Eagerness regained its hold on Dr. Brown. "Talk it over with your parents. Take a few days."

"I will, to be polite," I allowed. "But I'm going." From the moment I heard the proposition, my gut, heart and brain voted for acceptance. No second thoughts, no posing of doubts. This was an adventure, one bred by newsreels, movies, news stories and books about the war in Europe. With the war ended, it was time to go. All my young life had been a preamble for this moment. I knew it.

Dr. Brown regarded me with genuine fondness, his choice vindicated by my excitement and determination. I smiled confidently at him. I long ago learned the pose of maturity beyond my years. This trip offered no difficulties that I couldn't master.

That evening as I burst through the front door of our apartment, I discovered my parents and my younger sister Peggy awaiting me in nervous anticipation. My parents sat in silence while Peggy bent close to the radio, afraid to play it too loud for fear of breaking the spell. My arrival caused them all to rise to their feet as if attending royalty. "Did you hear?" I trilled in my tenor voice.

"Well, we talked to Dr. Brown," my mother said.

"The Gordon Brown Scholarship."

"Do you think you should take it?" my father tried.

"Why not?"

"The war is barely over," he began. "There are riots and strikes over there." The news he edited for his paper every day consumed his thoughts and reinforced his already pessimistic global view.

"Come on, Pop. Riots in Switzerland?"

"You have to get there. France is in turmoil. The Communists are trying there what they did in Poland."

"Communists don't worry me. We won the war and I won the scholarship." Maybe it was the tone of assurance, or the crooked smile I affected or the embrace that I gave my mom, but suddenly they were laughing and tousling my hair.

Peggy hugged me around the waist from behind and chanted, "Of everyone in the school they chose you. My own brother. They must not know what they're doing."

"It's not gonna cost you any extra money, is it, Pop? He said full scholarship."

"We pay transportation and keep you in beer and poker money."

"Carl! He's leaving home for Europe." My mother made the destination seem a distant planet of no return. "Alone. He's only fourteen."

"I'm an old fourteen, Ma. I grew up in Chicago, didn't I?"

"Don't accept simply because it was offered. There'll be time later in life to go to Europe."

"I'll think about it, Ma. Don't worry."

That night in bed with the lights out, I didn't stand a chance of sleeping. Instead, I tossed in a turmoil of excitement and pride, thrilled to the point of delirium over my good fortune. The faculty selection committee chose me from a school packed with bright students, some of whom were brilliant, like my buddy Mike Straus. Many of my mates were from prominent families, children of old money who lived in the last remaining mansions on Lake Shore Drive and who wore expensive clothing deliberately torn or ill-fitted in a laughable attempt to prove they were just plain folks. Some were the offspring of industrialists or speculators, entertainers or artists, some recent escapees from the war in Europe. Scholarship students of varying skin colors and heritages leavened the mix. From this exotic brew, I had been drawn before upperclassmen, dean's-list students and athletes.

"Are the Brackbirns solvent?" my father asked Dr. Brown a few days later when we gathered in his stuffy little garret. "Hank won't end up stuck over there if they go broke."

Dr. Brown waved away such notions, shooting a warning glance at my father against discussing material matters in front of a young scholar whose mind must remain fixed on the higher callings. "I'm told there will be 50 to 75 boarding students and almost as many day pupils. Those numbers should keep the Brackbirns solvent." He adopted a smug, don't-worry-your-little-head attitude as he picked up his personal file on the new school. With great satisfaction he weighed its heft in his plump hands. " I would never send a student over there without complete and total assurance from the Brackbirns that their school was financially sound and academically strong. It will be an educational crossroads where children from Europe, England and even Asia will gather in cultural accord. To me it sounds like a young person's version of the United Nations Organization, an acting out of the dream of a peaceful, stable world made whole by the next generation."

This discourse from the learned principal overwhelmed my parents. My mother gave a smile of relief, and my father, a professional doubter, turned to me with the air of a man who reluctantly accepts an argument.

"What language do they speak in Switzerland?" Peggy asked one night shortly after my anointment.

"Several," I bluffed. I was pretty sure of French and German but I didn't relish sounding uncertain so soon after receiving this honor.

"Swiss German and French," my mothered offered.

My father, usually the final authority on factual matters, gazed off into the middle distance. "Italian too, I believe."

"Italian? No." Peggy's seventh-grade education had not included this bit of knowledge.

"Let's look it up to be sure," my father announced. Peggy groaned. Now it was a family project. We would all be forced to read the encyclopedia and library books on Switzerland, then be oppressed by my father's verbal quizzes. Sure enough, he herded us to the precious books of knowledge. We pored over the pages until dizzy from forced information.

The new school was located in a French-speaking canton of Switzerland. Naturally, French would be a primary object of study. This captivated my father, whose ancestry, an incongruous and unlikely European blend of several warring powers including France, Germany and England, had been scoured by the process of Americanization. The idea of his only son conversing in the language of his ancestors, as well as of statesmen and diplomats, lured him from his customary rationality. One Sunday after all of us had concluded a Swiss study session, my father puffed himself up to proper proportions as head of household and announced with all the assurance at his command, "When Hank comes back, we will speak nothing but French at home."

There followed a stunned silence. That no one could speak a word of French placed no impediment in the path of a man who desired only the most sophisticated education possible for his family.

At school, word spread with the speed of tribal drums. Then to affirm the appointment, one day at Morning Exercise, Dr. Brown rose to announce the first recipient of the Gordon Brown Scholarship. "We know that Mr. Hank Douglas will represent his family, this school, city and country as the best his generation has to offer. Please join me in bidding him Godspeed and bon voyage for his impending journey." Then he stepped back from the microphone to lead the school in applause, which quickly evolved into my buddies' chanting my name. I couldn't help but note their tone of mockery, but when they pushed me to my feet, I stood and waved my arms, my ears aflame with embarrassment and pride.

Billy Curtis pulled me aside during baseball practice in the gym—it was too cold and rainy on the field. "At least they picked a gentile. Not a sheenie like Straus."

"Don't start it," I warned. Curtis had lately acquired a nasty tone regarding race and nationality.

"I hope your voice changes before you go. Otherwise those French whores won't believe you can do it." Curtis howled at his insight and ran off to tell Otto Minkus, our shortstop, his latest bit of wisdom.

My girlfriend, Joy Moody, showed a curious reserve about my selection. It puzzled me until we went to a Friday night party at Mike Straus's townhouse. We shuffled in the dark with our arms around each other as Frank Sinatra crooned "Laura." Joy whispered, "Hank, I can't do things with you just because you're going overseas. It's not like you're a GI and this is your last night."

"Of course not."

"As long as you understand."

I stroked her hair and whispered soothing comforts. Although I hadn't considered my departure in those terms, I suffered a true letdown. I was crossing an ocean and plunging into an alien land. Surely some sort of farewell gesture from the opposite sex wouldn't have been out of place. But my sex life remained talk and fantasy. I knew what men were supposed to do—the precocious kids at school had detailed the male role with examples from their experiences. But my voice hadn't yet deepened into manhood, much to my chagrin.

Joy, however, seemed more than satisfied with our swaying on the dance floor and clumsy petting on the couch. Things would be different for me in Europe, where sex is a part of everyday life. Adolescent boys in Europe don't remain immature very long, at least according the European literature and Hemingway stories I had pulled from my father's bookshelves.

Meanwhile, my father, surely at the urging of my mother, undertook a fateful man-to-man about the subject that quite literally embarrassed him to tears. Not long before I was to board the train for New York City where the ocean liner *De Grasse* awaited, my father approached me in my bedroom. From the man's agonized expression and fit of fidgets I sensed the topic.

"I guess I don't have to tell you anything about anything, do I?" he began. Not to torture him but unsure what to answer, I remained quiet. "A boy your age at a progressive school, you must know all about it."

"About what?"

"Girls. Women."

"You mean sex?"

Tears welled as he grabbed his stomach, the pain intense

on hearing that word spoken by a family member. "Do you have any questions?"

"Not really." His discomfort was too extreme to be enjoyed.

"You probably know more about it than I do."

"'I say, Carl. That's not cricket.'" I mimicked the expression of one of his tennis-playing friends from the British consulate.

For a moment he was unsure whether I was ridiculing him or not. But then we exchanged that private glance, the one that preceded the big wink. He threw an arm around my shoulder, gave a squeeze, then left to tell his wife their boy was ready to take on the world.

Simply traveling to New York City alone by train would have been an adventure. But the fact that it was only a minor leg on a major journey made it seem a simple commute. Nevertheless, at Union Station in Chicago, my family surrounding me, the train trip took on great significance. Perspiration from the hot summer day gave my mother an excuse to dab at her eyes with her handkerchief. My sister repeatedly called attention to the passing scene—"Look, he's got a cat in that box." Or, "She's wearing a fur and it's August"—as though to avoid the inevitable departure. My father, who often raised one arm protectively across my back when crossing the street to shield me from unseen attackers—sometimes he even grabbed my hand even when I was old enough to resent being treated as a child—now barely touched me. Only at the proper time did he extend his hand for a manly shake.

I was cut loose. My mother's tears on my cheeks. Peggy's frantic squeeze still tight on my ribs. My father's mature grip imprinted on my hand. As I gazed out the window at them on the platform, an odd relief overbore a sense of sadness. I was out of the nest with no one to answer to. Unconsciously I stretched as if spreading my wings.

THE SEA OF CLOUDS

Day coach. Sitting up for the 18-hour haul to the world's greatest port city. A brown-bag meal packed by my mother relieved me of the expense of the dining car. A newsman friend of my father met me at Penn Station in Manhattan, ensconced me in a modest hotel downtown, and then rushed me on a lightning tour of the great city. Times Square alight with theaters and movie palaces where the Mills Brothers, Gene Krupa and his band, and Frankie himself at the Paramount performed between movie showings. The street struggles of new postwar cars contending with the old pre-war cabs, built to specification for the city and as solid and durable as the tanks that had rolled over the Nazi army in France and Germany.

The whirl, the hustle and my lack of sleep from the train ride left me in a daze of lights, motion and sound. Falling into my bed that night, I passed out without removing my clothes, and but for a mistaken call to my room by the desk clerk, I would have slept through my sailing time.

Flights to Europe existed only for the wealthy. Ocean liners were the usual means of transatlantic travel. The Hudson River waterfront entertained as much shipping traffic as Broadway did cars. Standing at the railing of the *De Grasse*, I saw passenger liners, freighters, cruise ships, ferries, tugs lashed to barges full of goods and garbage. The river churned and lapped with the wakes of powerful vessels. Boat whistles filled the air as the docks and piers on both sides of the river burst with activity, spilling over into tenders, launches and dinghies.

The harbor pulsed and surged, pumping and heaving like a vibrant organism. Even under the relentless August sun at high noon, a chilling thrill shimmered through my body. Here I was, a part of this fantastic energy, a kid being swept out to sea toward his mission in Europe. I all but sang as tears filled my eyes. This was what I had imagined the trip would be like. This was adventure and derring-do. This was what being awarded the Gordon Brown Scholarship meant.

The blasting of steam horns, assertive yet plaintive, signaled departure. The mighty ship was eased into the frantic harbor by muscular tugs, and soon we were cruising past the Statue of Liberty, this time lifting her torch in farewell rather than welcome.

The *De Grasse* proved to be a chunk of France broken away from the Continent to ply the Atlantic passenger routes. From the rich, delectable meals to the brusque manner of the staff, this was the Old World. The lower depths where my cabin was located bred the heavy odor of mildew, stale corridors and diesel fumes. The whiff of disinfectant from multitudinous episodes of seasickness cleansings was accompanied by the pungent hum of generators. Stewards, in starched, threadbare white linen jackets, hurried along the stuffy passageways in their practiced sea gait. My cabinmate turned out to be a Rhodes scholar headed to Oxford for a year.

"You going to Southampton?" I asked.

"Of course."

"I'm going to Le Havre so you take the bunk by the door. You get off first."

He assumed the quizzical expression I knew so well. The half-smile that recognized the lame joke. Dry humor was the polite label given by people wishing to be kind.

Underway, the venerable ship creaked, moaned and cried, protesting its age and long service. On an upper deck, the dining hall held the perfume of musky table wine, olive oil, garlic, baking bread. Water was poured from a deep green Vichy bottle. The cheese service following the meal was ample enough for a lunch back home.

"May I have a glass of milk?" The waiter recoiled with

such shock, eyebrows that shot up, a hasty shake of the head, a studious aversion of the eyes, that I knew never to ask again. I filled my glass with red wine from the bottle on the table, but one sip brought on a gagging fit. One of my tablemates, an elderly Frenchman with a gray goatee yellowed with nicotine and the sallow skin and watery eyes of experience, poured most of the wine from my glass into his, then mixed the rest with water. "To begin," he said.

Passengers ate with the fork held upside-down in the left hand, knife at the ready in the right. Torn between remaining true to my American heritage and the urge to be accepted as a European, I ended up eating the European way. But I silently vowed that I would never mimic the French boys in fashion. At my age most still wore short pants like little kids, with shirts buttoned at the neck, neckties and long dark stockings. None sported white athletic socks, Levi's or khakis, our mandatory uniform. They cut their hair short at the ears and let the top grow long like a rag mop. I would keep my crew cut: like the khakis, an homage to the GI's.

I showed off my Ping-Pong skills, certain I would prevail in the ship's tournament. My confidence soared when I met my first-round opponent, a French boy about my age who wore the ridiculous outfit. We shook hands and exchanged a few words in pidgin French and English. I felt sorry for the guy. He held the racket like a girl, as if he were going to write with it rather than swing it. He skipped from one side of the table to another, his silly hair bobbing like an ill-fitting wig. I would be gracious in triumph.

Then the game began and he was all over the place, returning shots I thought I had put away and serving with a spin on the ball that I struggled to return. I wondered why he wasn't more deferential to me as a representative of the nation that had rescued him from the Nazis. As I was contemplating, he was playing and winning. I shook his hand, being gallant in defeat, but he gushed to me in his broken English. "I am good, no?"

"No," I responded. "I mean, yes, you are good."

I enjoyed the immense relief of knowing that the guys at Hillard would never hear about my losing to a kid who looked like that. And named Pierre, of all things. But I became close to Pierre and found myself cheering for him to win the championship, which he did. As the warm days rolled by, he became a good traveling companion. We explored the ocean liner, especially those areas that were off-limits, seeking refuge in empty stowage when threatened with discovery by passing crewmembers.

"The enemy comes," he said in English when we were on the verge of being found where we shouldn't have been.

"*Sacrebleu!*" I gasped, and we clenched to stifle our giggles.

Then, early one morning, out of the mist emerged the green hills of Ireland. After days of nothing but seascapes, the sudden interjection of land startled like a verdant iceberg for which the ship was headed. Not long afterward the white cliffs of Dover appeared in all their massive majesty, and soon the angular loading cranes in the harbor of Southampton were swinging across our bow like giant ravenous insects.

The crossing to Le Havre, which the crew and other veteran travelers warned could be treacherous, turned out to be pleasant. But as the Continent made itself known, I witnessed firsthand a scene straight from the wartime newsreels. Half-sunken ships littered the inlet at Le Havre, supply ships, landing craft and a few armored fighting ships. Barbed wire coiled on the beaches, awaiting the assault. Behind them huddled Nazi pillboxes and antiaircraft emplacements, their weapons still in place. The war could have been in full swing, lacking only bullets and explosions.

This was the reality that I had only imagined as we played war games in the park. Running across the grass with wooden slats as rifles. Belly flopping, then taking aim at anything in our way. Gunfire and bombs percussioned from our lips, spittle flying like shrapnel. We rose to lunge our bayonets into the wounded enemy, screaming our vengeance and triumph.

American boys slaying the hated Hun and Jap. Brave, fearless, stalwart. American. A nation unlike any other in the history of the human race, we were peace-loving until attacked. Then we turned our national fury on our tormentors. The boys would lead the way. Order would be restored. None of us doubted this and the fervor of our war games reflected it, whether in the city park or alone in the foxhole I had dug in a field near my grandmother's house in Wisconsin.

After what resembled hand-to-hand combat with the porters at the boat train who exuded the savage gleam of cannibals about to lower a new victim into a boiling pot, I got my meager possessions onto the train. Then in Paris the same scene was repeated, Gare St. Lazare to Gare de Lyon. Memorized polite French phrases fled my brain in the fracas. Francs for tips ripped from my sweaty palms. My arms ached from clinging to my luggage, which was under constant assault. By the time I piled on the train for Neuchâtel, I was a mess of contradictions, proud of my raw European conquest of the train transfer and distressed at my inability to command in the French tongue. That will soon change, I pledged as I settled in for my rendezvous with Josh Brackbirn.

Chapter Two

I had an idea of what Josh would look like from his photograph in the school's brochure. His distinguishing feature, however, was the broad, optimistic smile that highlighted his face. But the gaunt, dark-complexioned young man standing on the platform, whom I guessed was he, bore only a passing resemblance to the photo. Instead, he appeared glum, slightly bored and very impatient. He didn't even raise his eyes to examine the departing passengers. I approached him cautiously, unwilling to make a fool of myself by greeting a complete stranger.

"Josh?"

"Yes."

"It's me." I smiled so hard my cheeks ached.

"It is, is it?" He betrayed no emotion as he withheld his hand.

His slack posture and seeming preoccupation made the excitement of my adventure crumble.

"Hank Douglas. Chicago." I tried.

"I know, I know," he said. Then, like the sun breaking through stubborn storm clouds, his face brightened and he thrust his hand toward me. "Welcome to civilization."

I grasped his hand with fervor. He had made me run the gamut from joy to uncertainty followed by gratitude in a matter of nanoseconds. It wouldn't be the only time Josh worked his special necromancy on me.

"Good journey?" Josh asked, but before I could answer, he

grabbed my Val-a-Pak, freshly festooned with steamship and train decals, and strode ahead.

"I have a trunk that was checked."

"Do you? I might have suspected."

With great dispatch we boarded a tram that carried us to the funicular railroad, while he declaimed about his school. "We expect students from various countries, a true crosscutting of the civilized world. Your days of insular life are finished. You will be the wiser and better man for it."

The description rivaled that given me by Dr. Brown. But being delivered here, in Switzerland, added authenticity. When he referred to me as a man, I puffed with pride. I was a man on a man's mission in spite of my boyish physical limitations. Josh and I would share life's experiences man to man.

When the tram halted at the funicular, the two of us unloaded my goods and stood before the station. Josh announced, "The ride up will be the experience of a lifetime, I assure you."

"This is just ... great!" Without thinking, I threw an arm around his shoulder in a display of camaraderie.

"I say. None of that." He took a hasty step away from me as if I had touched him with a diseased hand.

The funi car ran up a single track, hauled by a thick cable that snaked along between the rails. The car was a compact steel-and-glass capsule with a couple of short rows of wooden seats. As on the tram, passengers greeted each other as if old friends. But this fraternization tapered off, and it became obvious that they were strangers being polite. Posters on the walls of the funi station proclaimed the upcoming *fête de la vendange*, as grinning workers in bright work clothing, their cheeks bursting with the bloom of health, toted wicker baskets of just harvested grapes to wooden vats and bottles of new wine dotted the margins. I asked

Josh what that meant and he replied, "The wine festival. Care to tie a bun on, would you?" He laughed at the thought.

The posters for the wine festival, the Swiss passengers, some of the men in dark-blue smocks and work pantaloons that gathered at their ankles above hobnailed boots, the funi car poised for the ascent like the ultimate ride in a huge natural amusement park—nothing in the Midwest matched this, and for all I knew or cared, nothing anywhere on earth came close.

Josh positioned me beside him facing the rear window. When I twisted to face uphill, he spun me back without a word. After the clang of a bell and the clattering close of the sliding doors, the car gave a lurch then started its slow, methodical ascent. The hillside glided silently beneath us, and soon we plunged into a swirl of clouds that denied us any view of the landscape. "Will it be like this the whole way?" I asked.

"Be patient," Josh said. His restrained air packed a sense of surprise. A treat awaited me if I could but hold on for it to arrive. I bounced on the balls of my feet, excitedly waiting for the clouds to clear. Halfway up, the single track bowed into a bypass and another funi car slipped past us. Passengers in both cars read or even dozed during the trip as if on the familiar commuter el back home. Hadn't Josh told them what was in store?

Then as if in answer to my silent question, our funi car burst out of the cloud bank into the slanted rays of the afternoon sun. Behind us swept the Alps, mantled with snow even in September, arrayed across the far reaches of the nation to define its borders. "Not bloody much like Chicago, would you believe?" Josh said with an edge of superiority.

"Wow, not at all. Wow!"

"Wow, eh?" Josh mimicked. "We'll put some proper words in your mouth before we're done. Rest assured of that."

Josh began to tick off some of the more prominent peaks, which resonated with the force of the solemn passwords of a secret cult. Matterhorn. Jungfrau. Mont Blanc. The names tripped off his tongue as if he visited them every day. The dunes of Michigan and the hills of Wisconsin were but pimples of land compared with these broad-shouldered, white-topped monsters. They beckoned, invited exploration and drew me toward them, away from the cozy world of safe sanity. The mass of roiling clouds lapped on the shores of the Alps, and stretched across Switzerland to nestle at the base of the hills above Neuchâtel.

"What do they call it?"

"The Sea of Clouds. Only the most lofty rise above it." His tone made clear his belief that he was among the lofty, an attainment others could only dream of reaching.

As we rolled upward past the mist and into the clear air, the long rays of the lowering sun cast the Alps in a hue of ancient brass. The tiny car hauled us on its narrow track, gliding through the tree-carpeted mountainside. The vertical surge defied gravity, and I experienced the distinct sensation of leaving behind the world of flatlanders and common sense.

Lost in my solitary reverie, I gave an involuntary start when Josh spoke in my ear. "Bloody impressive, what?"

"Bloody right," I affirmed. Josh and I snorted little laughs. I enjoyed the sound of us in harmony. I basked in his favor, certain I had misjudged his earlier dark mood. He was a European, not a high school kid from home. I had expected another type of person.

As we turned up the rough road leading to the school, the château on the hillside materialized like a castle from a golden time. I had seen its photograph in the school brochure, but it transcended its reproduced image. Involuntarily, I halted, brought up short by the sight. The façade, with its ornate eaves, bay windows and fronting balconies, could have been fashioned of gingerbread. A slate roof was set against a rich green curtain of evergreens. Most important, the fairytale château exuded welcome and peace. If it were a person, it would have opened its elegant arms to comfort the enthralled traveler.

A broad flagstone terrace bordered by low stone walls commanded a view facing east to the Alps. There awaited Lily, Josh's mother and the headmistress of the school. She was a small woman with a shy smile that lent her a girlish quality. Her teeth, oversize as though intended for a larger person, and forefingers bore nicotine stains from the French cigarettes that she smoked constantly. Her light smoker's cough, I soon learned, served as a warning of her presence when she was out of sight. Her chestnut hair, swept up in a stylish bun, evinced no traces of gray. Indeed, she appeared quite young for a woman who had suffered the displacements of war and now ran a school on a foreign mountainside.

With her guarded smile, diminutive stature and youthful air, Lily seemed an older sister rather than a stern headmistress. Without thinking, I raised my arms to hug her. Her face hardened, she stepped back and said tightly, "You'll be sleeping upstairs with the other boys."

"Great! Where are they?"

She regarded me with suspicion, placed her cigarette in her mouth, gave her signature cough, and walked away. Her shoulders were slightly rounded, her steps as short and measured as a little girl's.

I found a wheelbarrow and rolled my possessions from the funi station to the château. I lugged my Val-a-Pak then my footlocker up the stairs and entered the room I was told was the boys' dormitory. As I unrolled a mattress onto a cot and began to make the bed with sheets I had brought with me, I wondered why the other cots were unmade, their mattresses rolled up. I assumed the other boys were quartered elsewhere. I poked around in the other rooms. No sign of anyone else. All the cots bore a curled-up mattress, and the rooms echoed with the lack of humans.

I sat slumped on my cot, alone. A hand bell sounded without accompanying instructions. I eased onto the stairs and peered down. Lily and Josh stood silently at the dining room table, sipping tea. Unsure if this were a private ritual, I feared to ask instructions. But as I hovered on the stairs, Josh said, without turning his head in my direction, "Care for tea?"

"Me?"

"Do you see anyone else?"

"No. I mean, sure I'd like some tea." Besides tea, there was a wedge of fresh black bread and a small pot of honey that I shared with the boy-headmaster and his mother. No one else. So aloof were the Brackbirns that it pained me to inquire, "Are the others due soon?"

"All things in their time," Josh answered. "The pound sterling is blocked in England, as you may or may not know. The war left us destitute." I pressed him for more intelligence. But his tone shifted to administrator. "English is permitted at teatime. French at tea would be an abomination. But we shall speak only French at meals."

Recalling my father's pronouncement that on my return our family would speak only French at home, I gave a brief laugh.

"I say, you can be a bit of a twit. I trust this shan't be a sign of your capacities as a student."

"I'm sorry. I don't know any French. But I'll learn. I swear."

"Never mind." Again his clouded face broke into a sunny smile. "Long journey. Still a child." He examined me as if unsure whether to keep me or return me to the store. "Dear me."

I embarked on a long walk into the woods. As I wandered, I affirmed that my main goal was to accept my plight as worthy. I told myself the trip would be worth these few moments of disappointment. But after a brief supper during which only French was permitted, the cabbage and boiled potatoes congealed in a tough, greasy wad in my gut. I gazed out the window of the boys' dorm. I was overseas, alone and scared. My wartime movies played out their pitiful drama of fear spawned by distance from the known world and imposed isolation.

As I lay awake that first night, alone in the cavernous dormitory, the stripped empty bunks with their coiled mattresses taunted my lofty expectations. I was trapped in a château with a decidedly odd couple of strangers. The pain of this heightened a racking bout of homesickness that left me too absorbed for tears.

I began plotting my escape. But to where? If I retreated home, I would have cost my parents a small fortune in travel tickets. I'd be an object of jibes at Hillard, which in its own way would be worse than toughing it out. What line had the Brackbirns given Dr. Brown that he accepted without question? I won the first Gordon Brown Scholarship. "Thank you for the honor. And thank you for the gift of the Black Plague. It was exactly what I needed."

I longed to cry; yet I feared that the Brackbirns would hear me. Something about their superior attitude drove me to defy them. I would never display any vulnerability lest they hold it up to ridicule. My anger at them for their tall tales about the school gave me no leeway for charity. They dragged me over here with false promises. Now I was caught, too proud to flee, too confused to be reasonable. I pulled my pillow over my face and held my breath. God would recognize this act of desperation and whisk me back to Chicago.

In the morning, I awoke early and pulled a writing pad and a pen from my footlocker.

Dear Mom and Pop,

I'm at school at last, and it isn't at all what I expected. Guess what? I'm the only student. That's right. Only me. The Brackbirns seem quite nice. At least they can be. But they are British and kind of hard to talk to. They say there is no money in England or Europe to run a school. But we knew that before I came over. I guess they only just found out.

Right now I'm very lonely and homesick, and I think this trip may have been a huge mistake. I feel trapped here with a very strange couple, mother and son, who don't even talk much to each other. Can you get me out of here as soon as possible? I know this will have cost you a lot of money. I'm so sorry about that. I'll make it up to you someday. But right now I feel like I'll go crazy if I stay here. I'm kind of young to go to a loony bin, although I may already be in one.

I'm sorry this didn't work out. I know I insisted I go against your advice. But it's done and I'm ready to call it quits and take the blame. Please write to me soon and tell me when and how I can get out of here.

Love,
Hank

As I slipped the letter into an airmail envelope, I felt relieved. The very act of writing had restored a fresh resolve to face the Brackbirns and their school. I put the letter into my footlocker, ready to mail if things didn't change.

To escape the Brackbirns, I busied myself with solitary exploration of the surrounding hillside, where I sat and studied the views of the Alps. These sights alone were reason enough for the trip abroad. And at any given time, the evanescent Sea of Clouds would roll across the country, introducing an eerie chill to the majestic scene. Like Josh, the landscape shifted its mood at random, casting its spell with a suddenness that surprised and startled.

THE SEA OF CLOUDS

In the rare moments the Brackbirns spoke, they made no effort to link me with Hillard School and their years in Chicago. Then one morning after breakfast, Josh leaned back in his chair, placed his hands behind his head and asked in English, "How is our old friend Ellis?"

Stunned at this sudden inquiry about a favorite faculty member, I responded with the startled mumble of a student caught napping in class.

"He was one of the few professors there who bore a scintilla of intelligence. Yes, Ellis is salvageable. But the others." Josh closed his eyes, appearing on the verge of sleep. "Except, of course, Dr. Brown. Not a brilliant man, but one with vision. Even you must realize that."

"Yeah. Vision," I repeated.

"Had the foresight to sponsor and endorse our educational institution. Helped us immeasurably. He is aware, within his capacities, of what we are accomplishing here." Josh lowered his chair and dropped his elbows onto the table. His eyes remained shut. "The students work hard here." He made it sound as though a massive student body toiled in the château even as he spoke. "Rigorous classes and assignments that keep them up well into the night. Read the English masterpieces from the finest books and instructors available on the Continent. It tests their will. But they *learn*."

Not one to shy away from a challenge, I said, "As they should."

"Good boy," Josh opened his eyes and smiled. "That's the spirit."

I grinned like a child given a pat on the head. My hopes rose when we hit it off. Even more encouraging, there followed a reminiscence of Josh's years in Chicago. "Chicago proved a pleasant shock," he allowed. "After the long months of bombardment it was a needed comfort with its obliviousness and mindless population." He delivered this last judgment with a wink and a crooked smile, sharing a joke with me. We were becoming buddies. I spent the rest of that day convinced I had been too harsh in my judgment. After all, his school, so effusively touted, had no enrollment. He was gambling and losing. I gave him every benefit of the doubt. I wished for nothing less than for everyone to get along. Now I was sure we would. I congratulated myself for not mailing the letter to my parents.

The following morning I greeted Josh like a pal with a cheery *"Bonjour!"* The boy-headmaster did not lift his eyes from his book. Several other attempts in my original style of French led nowhere. I downed my coffee and bread in morose silence. Even Lily's appearance couldn't pry a word from him.

After breakfast Josh, bearing two thick volumes, bore down on me. "Read these to start you off properly for the term." He thrust the books forward with the satisfaction of one who has delivered a body blow to an antagonist. I scanned the titles. One concerned great English literature, the other a collection of plays by Molière, in French. The markings showed it had been borrowed from a public library in London and not returned. "Now your education begins," Josh announced, his attention on the briar pipe he could never keep lit.

Mealtime brought out the worst in the Brackbirns. The three of us sat at the long, broad dining room table—a table groaning for a noisy, hungry crowd—engaged in a tense language game. The Brackbirns were accomplished in French vocabulary, yet their accents left no doubt as to their country of origin. So Anglo-Saxon were their tone and cadence that I could almost follow their discussion by their speech patterns alone.

Nor were they concerned with my comprehension. In fact, they enjoyed using French to exclude me. They traded insider sentences, punctuating them with sly glances to reaffirm that I was lost. During these episodes, I acted the student. I smiled when they did, nodded foolishly and added knowing chuckles when it seemed appropriate. I even picked up some Gallic gestures, shrugs and emphatic honks to show I was trying. But I couldn't learn by emulating them. They were neither native nor genuine. Instead I vowed to master French so that when the locals wished to illuminate a subtle point, they would turn to me for my command of the language of diplomats.

Skilled manipulators, the Brackbirns sensed exactly when I had had enough—a foolish stuttering, the flash of anger in my eyes. Then they would drop all pretenses. Smile at me in the friendliest manner. Say some words of encouragement in exaggerated French that even a dullard could grasp. Naïf to the core, I pledged to work harder at the language.

Of all the disturbing habits of the Brackbirns, one grated more than all the others combined. Josh kept an aging setter named Pancho. He paid scant attention to the dog, seldom petted him and spoke to him only when he sought to address someone else. Such as, "Hank has his elbows on the table, Pancho. Tell him we're not in America now. Civilized people have proper table manners." Overjoyed to hear his name from his master's lips, Pancho would slap his tail in gratitude on the tile floor of the dining room and raise his muzzle awaiting the comforting pat that never came.

Josh did more than ignore the dog, however. He waited until Pancho settled close to his feet, then he would cross his legs catching the old dog in the flank with his shoe. Sometimes this sneak attack missed, but more than once Pancho yelped or whined as he spun around in confusion. Annoyed as though it were the dog's fault, Josh would mutter, "I say, Pancho. Can't a person cross his legs without a tiresome commotion?"

These soft kicks were so nonchalant, at first I didn't believe they were intentional. Even Josh wouldn't be that gross and obvious. But this cruel ritual occurred too frequently to be accidental. At last, I objected in English. "Hey, you're kicking the dog."

"*Parlez français à table, s'il vous plaît,*" Josh answered.

My first days at school repeated this debilitating pattern. A few caring, pleasant words from my hosts lifted my spirits and outlook, the taciturn growls at the table or the brief yelp of the poor dog underfoot would ignite a controlled fury in me. I lectured myself that these people were administrators and teachers, not buddies from home. We weren't supposed to pal around together. I could espouse this solemn, adult view that was one of my strengths. But adhering to it as a steady diet proved trying. "Hell," I reminded myself. "I'm a 14-year-old kid, not a damn grown-up."

Chapter Three

At teatime a savior materialized on the terrace: a young male human. Someone who wasn't Josh or Lily. The newcomer was weird, all right. His red hair hung waxen and lank, his eyes pink as a lab rat's, his woolen bell-bottoms and double-breasted suit coat sagged on his gaunt frame.

"Are you a student?" I asked. I feared that the guy was a stranger the Brackbirns had brought in for appearances' sake.

"Yes, actually. My name is Anthony Joseph Heath-Merriweather. My mother is very rich and distinguished."

Now that was a European introduction. "Will you be here for the year?"

"I should imagine. Are you an American?"

"No. I'm native Swiss."

Tony eyed me before announcing, "A wise guy, I take it."

I noticed Josh and Lily pretending not to watch from behind the dining-room French doors as I recanted. "Yeah, I'm American."

"Do you have gangs here? Being an American, I mean, you must have gangs and rumbles and all sorts of excitement."

"I'm the only kid here. But I'm a one-man gang."

Again the new boy's eyes clouded over with puzzlement, then he let out a heavy laugh. "Well said! A one-man gang. I shall have to remember that."

The newcomer clipped off a few tight strides as though completing a small square of march commanded by a superior.

Not eager to push too hard at first, I slipped back into the dining room to pour some tea.

"I see we have another student." I affected a casual air as though this arrival was nothing special.

"Expected him yesterday. Bloody awful conditions still. The war, in case you forgot."

"Help Anthony with his luggage," Lily said at me. She never called me by name, the same vagueness of address employed with the Italian maids. Since they seldom knew whom she was talking to or why, they ended up staring at each other gulping air, eyes as glassy as freshly landed fish.

Anthony and I dropped his trunk in the dorm, and he fell onto the springs of the cot near the door. The mattress unrolled and flopped over his legs. "I fancy being near the door. Don't like to be crowded, in point of fact."

"How old are you?"

"Fifteen, coming up for sixteen. Stand by," Anthony said. He tore open his footlocker and dug in. Ugly wool clothes and heavy suit coats spilled out. "Being an American, you must have seen things then held your tongue."

"I can keep a secret, if that's what's bothering you."

"This is more than a secret. It could lead to a jolly good caning."

"I'm not afraid of a caning." I wasn't too sure what a caning was. "I'm from Chicago."

The name of the city acted like a cord tightened around Anthony's neck. His face flushed, eyes bulged and his knees sagged. "Truly?"

"Born and raised there." I flipped open my wallet. An official-looking card showed under the dulled celluloid window. "My pass for Chicago buses. Use it every morning to get to school."

That cinched it. Someone from Chicago would understand. Anthony dove back into his trunk and found what he was after. "There!" He thrust a pistol at me. I began to object, but the responsibility of my Chicago heritage silenced me.

"It's only a Colt .22, mind you. Not a Luger or a Mauser or a Walther. I covet desperately a double-action P.38 Walther. But you no doubt own one. Do you?" I shook my head. "This will serve. I should love a shoulder holster. But this could rub someone out."

"It's not loaded, is it?"

"What kind of jerk do you take me for?" He cast a dubious glance at me to see if he sounded tough enough. "I sleep with it under my pillow."

"How did you get an American pistol?" I asked. "Isn't it illegal to have handguns in England?"

The new arrival adopted the blank face that was his primary refuge and continued his chores without comment. Watching Anthony Joseph Heath-Merriweather unpack that late afternoon redeemed for me the long lonely wait for another student. Among the highlights in his trunk were a dozen or so caps—leather, suede, wool—and several natty hats with little feathers jutting from them. Anthony tried on each as he drew it from his trunk. Also retrieved were ties still knotted that had been pulled off over his head and unlaundered dress shirts, webbed with wrinkles, collars bent and jutting at grotesque angles. Black wing tips, the heels worn over, dropped onto the bare floor. He also fished out a huge midnight-blue overcoat with aggressively pointed lapels and a belt. Everything had been thrown into the trunk helter-skelter, as though Anthony had been given five minutes to pack and clear out.

I watched enthralled as he wrestled on the huge overcoat and pulled the belt tight around his waist. He jammed onto his head a dark hat with a tan- and-yellow feather peeking from its band. He was an extra from a gangster movie. All he lacked was George Raft by his side and a five-o'clock shadow on his jowls rather than fuzzy blond down. He hunched his shoulders to adjust the pads of the coat and fixed his beady eyes on me.

"Call me Tough Tony, ya mug. What's funny?" Tony's facial muscles tightened to set his jaw at a menacing angle. He moved his hand inside his coat. Right in, right out. I caught the glint of gunmetal. Two sharp reports were accompanied by a narrow wisp of smoke. Then two more shots and a small shard of gray paper floated down to Tony's feet. "You're dead, ya rat."

The smile remained locked on my face. Tony whipped the cap pistol back inside his bulky overcoat and rubbed his pale hands together in anticipation. The dusk turned chilly in the dormitory.

"I shall want to live in America soon. Perhaps even Chicago. England is too bloody tame. Well?" Tony paused for my critique.

"You'll slay 'em in Chi-town."

"Yes, perhaps I shall slay 'em in Chi-town. What a jolly good way to put it." Tony smiled and raised a finger to caress one of the larger pimples near his mouth.

After Tony came Dun, a strapping young man who resembled a French Resistance fighter. With his sharp Gallic features, jutting chin, piercing eyes and attire of gray tweed herringbone knickers, wool knee socks, mountain boots and dark turtleneck sweater, he appeared ready to help an Allied intelligence agent bury his parachute after a night drop behind enemy lines. Moving calmly while Nazi sentry dogs bayed nearby.

"Three chaps," I crowed. "The start of a real gang."

Dun moved his eyes from me to Tough Tony and back to me, then resumed his unpacking.

"Right-o," Tony chimed. "A real gang, like in Chi-town."

I wished Dun had been more supportive, even if he didn't mean it. His glances at us when I suggested we were a gang approached contempt. He didn't relish being included with a couple of boys younger than he.

The following morning another student appeared on the terrace with only a large, broken-down suitcase held together by a thick rope. He was Hermon, a short, slight Chinese boy with a shock of black hair held back by what seemed heavy applications of auto grease. His first words were "I haven't missed breakfast, have I?" Missing a meal proved to be a primal fear, and no quest was too great, no voyage too momentous if it meant acquiring food.

That afternoon a Citroën pulled up loaded to the rooftop and out stepped Ruthie, a girl about nine, with a single pigtail, haunting green eyes, and the confident carriage of a person accustomed to having things go her way. Her mother, when she emerged from behind the steering wheel, bore the same easy elegance that comes from having the best, from schools and tailors to food and habitations. My first thought was What in the world are those two doing here? They could have gone somewhere really nice.

Their passenger was a girl who looked about my age. "Hello, I'm Wendy Winner," she said. "Ruthie and her mother were nice enough to give me a ride from Zurich." Her hand, plump and warm in mine, didn't linger long. "I'd love to chat but I have to get settled. I must look a fright." I watched her disappear inside the château. A trifle pudgy but well coiffed and dressed, she reminded me of some of the girls at Hillard, bright-eyed, confident, self-absorbed. Without waiting for instructions, Dun carried a couple of the suitcases inside and up the stairs. I followed suit, while Tony and Hermon watched.

At lunch, the French-only rule was in effect, which Josh enforced with his full authority. In the silence—none of us except Dun spoke French—I couldn't help noticing the subtle shift in Josh. Now he had a student body, pathetically small with six living souls to teach and administer, but it gave his existence meaning. A calm settled over him as he expanded to fill his roles of dean and one-person faculty. He smiled often, spoke French slowly for our benefit and in general proved an amiable host.

The first days of the Swiss English Academy's initial academic term bore all the earmarks of a traditional school opening. Each student copied the class schedule off the wheeled blackboard. All students were to attend the main classes together, like English literature and French, even though our ages ranged from nine to sixteen. The few textbooks had to be shared. We students fell into a period of getting acquainted while pretending real concern about our studies. Absent now my afternoons of lonely walks through the woods and my enervating bouts of self-pity. Kids' voices filled the marvelous mansion. Lily even smiled through the suffocating fog of her French cigarettes. Josh abandoned his mind games with me and assumed the role of don and headmaster. He spoke down to his charges from the heights of his position.

Then, lending further credence to the fact that the Swiss English Academy was an institute of learning, a new faculty member appeared. After lunch on that first day, a distracted young guy stumbled into the dining room seeming lost and disoriented, his thick glasses atilt on his bulbous nose, his tie flapped over his left shoulder and his shirt buttons misaligned so that one side of his collar waved above its mate like a signal of distress. His lips were set in a vague smile, as if aware of his comic appearance and unable to resist the joke himself.

Josh knew the interloper. "Ah, Gillet. Welcome." Then

he announced to us, "Monsieur Gillet is the latest addition to our faculty. He is from the region and thus well versed in French, German and astronomy." How being from Neuchâtel bestowed knowledge of the heavens was not made clear. "He will be instructing some of you in French, the French speakers in German and all of you in astronomy. I expect you to reserve the utmost attention and respect for this learned member."

But rather than leave his charges with this display of importance, Josh held up his hands to quiet the crowd and began yet another explanation of the school's mandate. "What we are accomplishing here is the very model of modern Continental education. We have elected to instruct with small classes, practicing the tutorial system prevalent in the finest British institutions. This ensures quality education." He closed his eyes and swallowed exaggeratedly, as a great orator might before his summation. "This school is a source of great pride for the faculty and administration. It should be for you as well."

In the respectful silence that followed, no one stirred. For once Josh spoke from the heart. Then, out of nowhere, came a long, deep-throated belch from little Hermon, a noise so unexpected and sudden that it caused every eye in the room to rivet on him.

"Right-o," Hermon beamed. "Well said." Whether he was referring to Josh's speech or to his own burp wasn't clear.

Josh and his minuscule student body gaped in wonder at the Chinese boy. A few embarrassed snickers seeped out, but this brash collision of East meeting West proved impossible to comprehend.

"I shall take that as an affirmation," Josh said trying to regain the upper hand.

"Please do," Hermon assured.

"Well, in closing," Josh tried, but the kids were lost to him.

The belch had broken his spell. "Dismissed," Josh barked. As his students hurried from his presence, Josh's eyes lingered on Hermon, certain he had been had. My appreciation for Hermon soared.

Chapter Four

"The postman says that wine might run from the fountains," Dun said after mail call. Monsieur Montraux was of that most cautious type of mountain man who delivered our mail on his BSA motorcycle without a word in excess. "He says that if the harvest is as good as it seems, wine will flow from fountains."

Unsure if we were being put on, I dug out an old guidebook from the shelves of Josh's little library. Sure enough, I found a confirming passage that I read aloud that night in our dorm. "'Legend has it that in 1657 Henry II of Orléans, heir of the noble French family that owned the city of Neuchâtel, had thousands of gallons of local *vin rouge* run through the Griffin Fountain to celebrate his triumphal entrance.' There *is* a tradition," I told my new friends.

"It shall happen," Hermon piped. "Wine flowing like water. I shall bring my tin cup."

"We'll all bring tin cups," I crowed. "Tin cups for everyone," Tony echoed. "Tin cups! Tin cups!" We took up the chant until Josh barked at us from the library below and we fell into a stillness broken only by one of us whispering, "Tin cups," which prompted shared merriment.

As we prepared for the festivities on the first night of the wine festival, Josh appeared in our room. As usual, he tried to be one of the guys, but his dismissive tone couldn't be restrained. "On guard that those scamps in town don't take all you've got."

"We're not afraid," I told him. "We have our gang."

"Like Al Capone," Tony added.

"You chaps, like Capone?" Josh forced his most disparaging cackle. "What guff. Gang of twits is more like it."

Before I could object, Dun snapped, "Must be on our way. Off we go."

Josh gave a disapproving grunt and left the room.

"That guy can ruin a wine festival before it even begins," I said.

"We shall walk to town," Dun announced. Young Hermon groaned and slumped on his bed, but that constituted the only objection. Dun believed one should earn life's bounties. Walking down a mountainside to celebrate a festival paid your debt to the god of pleasure. Since I had been raised with more than a faint strain of that ethic, I agreed. Besides, disagreeing with Dun about anything struck me as foolish.

Only when we were well along on the brisk eight-kilometer descent did Tony remind us: "We forgot our tin cups." We hadn't executed our plan. If we had been dropped behind enemy lines and failed to carry out instructions, we might now be prisoners of war or even dead. When we arrived in town in a sweaty state of anticipation, we galloped to the fountain in the rue du Château and plunged our hands under the flowing spout to taste the liquid.

"You didn't believe that guff about wine running like water." I adopted the newsman's cynical tone that said I hadn't been duped, even though I had been the major retailer of the rumor.

"Now I suppose there shall be no naked women either," Hermon lamented in his piping voice. "I shan't fall in love."

We chipped in for a bottle of local white and drank it near the fountain. In the course of time, Tough Tony lurched up and down the street, one foot on the curb, the other in the gutter.

He ranted about getting "plugged in da gam" during the St. Valentine's Day massacre.

"That happened right near my school in Chicago. In a riding stable across the street."

"Did you hear the machine guns? See the bodies?"

"I hadn't even been born yet." Seeing Tony's deep disappointment, I added, "But we heard all about it from the neighbors. The older ones."

"By Jove! So we *are* like a Capone gang."

"Sure we are," I agreed. "Josh doesn't know what he's talking about."

Abuzz with the wine, we discussed ways of returning to school that would be special, our secret gang way. Then Dun made the suggestion that set us on our rendezvous with history. The more we discussed the possibility, the more excited we became. While we milled among the crowd and jumped to the rhythm of the street bands, our true excitement remained reserved for the trip home. Drinking wine and dancing paled in comparison to what we had determined to try.

We caught the last tram run for the three-kilometer jaunt to Coudre at the end of the line. The funi station was shuttered and locked. We hid in the shadows by the side of the road until the tram conductor shut off his lights and disappeared up the road toward home. We waited until all traffic in the area halted for the night. Dun led the way to the tracks, marching with his usual purpose and focus, leading by example. He swung up. In no time, all four of us were climbing, crawling like monkeys up the tilted railway in the pitch black.

The tracks started by hugging the ground, and we ascended by standing upright and stepping from cross tie to cross tie. But soon they rose above the slope, traversing the undulating mountainside on a trestle that soared upward, smoothly and steadily, independent of the swells, cuts and crevasses below. We bent over, clutching the tracks or ties in front of us to maintain balance. The darkness worked in our favor, since we couldn't see how high we teetered above the mountainside. But occasionally we sensed the tops of tall firs beneath us. We crawled scores of feet above the ground, suspended in the cool night air.

At places, the mountain rose to greet us, the pale presence of rock outcroppings nearby or a baby evergreen at eye level. But I couldn't be certain of their relationship to the ground. This injected the tension of adventure that also contributed nervous fatigue. I started to sweat, the climbing position awkward. Bent over, hands steadying as my booted feet stepped upward. The grade was steep, the uncertainty inducing a thrilling anxiety as we ascended in silence.

"Watch out!" A cry of alarm came from the darkness behind me.

"What happened?" I made my way down the tracks to squat on my hams. My feet trembled on the ties beneath me. My hands grasped the track.

"Hermon's fallen off." Dun's voice echoed from beneath the trestle.

"Dun?" I stretched across the tracks to peer into the darkness. A chill of panic rippled through me. I couldn't tell how high we were. I feared Hermon had slipped into the void with Dun following him.

"What the deuce is happening?" Tony called from up the grade.

"Dun?" In desperation I leaned so far over the tracks that when Dun straightened up we almost touched noses. The silliness of it released a burst of laughter.

"The boy is out cold."

I swung off the tracks, my feet slapping on a large rock.

Hermon lay curled up in a cleared area in a field of stones. "Is he all right?"

"Who can know?"

Tony's voice sounded right above us. "Where is everybody?"

"Down here. Hermon's fallen off."

"Bad luck. What shall we do?"

"They throw water on people in the movies," I said.

"Where's water up here?"

"Maybe a spring somewhere."

"Not bloody likely." Dun's voice had the asperity he used in class when Josh hurried his answers.

"Why don't we piss on him?" Tony suggested. "From up here the force would be equal to a *douche*."

The concept struck us dumb. Pissing on him didn't seem the noble way to revive a fallen comrade. But when I saw Hermon move I offered, "The three of us pissing on Hermon is worth a try."

The ploy worked. The kid groaned and sat up. "Is it teatime?" he asked as he moved his hand to his right eye.

"If you fell where these tracks are higher you'd go to the big teatime in the sky," I said.

"Jolly good!" Tony laughed above us. "The big teatime in the sky."

"You were going to piss on me."

"Were you awake all the time?" Dun demanded.

"I fell asleep while I was climbing. I fell into this patch of moss. It's bloody comfortable here."

"Are you hurt?"

"Not that I fancy. My right eye aches."

"Let's proceed. Long way to go yet," Dun ordered.

"Can't I stay here? Call me at teatime." Hermon said as he lay back in his newfound nest.

Dun jerked Hermon to his feet. Then he lifted until the boy clung to the tracks while kicking his feet in the air. With Tony pulling and Dun and me pushing, Hermon regained his climbing position.

"Sleep is the best bloody thing in the world," Hermon told Tony as we climbed. "I love to sleep. There's all you can eat when you sleep. Mail arrives by the sackload. You can't read *Sir Gawain* when you sleep. The words all become one and have no bloody meaning."

Again the mountainous terrain rose and fell beneath us like a restless ocean. The track remained steady, though, making its way toward the summit without pitch or yaw. Hermon's accident brought home the dangers that awaited a slip or miscalculation. My hands trembled from the force of clinging. My boots moved mechanically.

Hermon's fall from the funi tracks liberated him. His piping voice tinkled like a music box in the clear night. He spilled a melodic waterfall of words, some English, some French, some Shanghai-ese. None of these made any sense, but they blended to hypnotic effect. Once or twice I felt myself dozing off to the lyrical jingle. Tony let out a sharp cry. His attention had lapsed, and his foot had slipped between the ties, skinning his shin.

"You've been dreaming," Hermon explained to Tony. "The same thing happened to me, except I fell to the ground. That's why my right eye hurts."

We were strung out several ties apart taking a rest in the pitch black. Our voices broke brittle in the autumn darkness. A slice of moon hung distant and cold; the stars, weak and frigid, swooned in the crystal night.

"You can get hurt climbing. My right eye aches like hell."

"I didn't know you knew so many words, Hermon," I said.

"Well, I do." Then he lapsed into his chant, now louder

and more earnest since Hermon knew he was being heeded, the bell-like sounds chiming in the forest below.

The grade steepened as the tracks rose into the Chaumont station. I struggled forward, focused on conquering the grade. Rivulets of sweat trickled down my rib cage. My breath came in measured beats; a rhythm entrenched, my body responding to the challenge. I saw Dun swing off the tracks as they disappeared into the funi station at the summit, and in a few moments I did the same. We waited while Tony completed his ascent. Then Hermon stood on the tracks above us. He beat his chest, gave a jungle yell like Tarzan and leapt toward us without warning. Only Dun's reflexive catch prevented him from crashing face-first into the ground.

This final daredevil act by Hermon gave us a fresh jolt of adrenalin. I grabbed the back of his neck in an affectionate squeeze. Then I punched Tough Tony lightly on the shoulder and shook Dun's meaty hand.

The white-dusted Alps loomed as pale specters lost in a far corner of the globe. The moon made the night glow with pale luminescence. We stood in its wash, alive and proud, the conquerors of our little mountain. I extended my right hand and took Hermon's. Dun placed his hand on top, while Tony added his. "We've done something never done before," I said. "No one can ever take this from us."

"Good luck to all of us," Dun said.

We resumed our attack on the mountain, this time strolling up the country road that led past the observation tower with its long runway access. The store—post office building was swallowed by the shadows. Hermon held a hand to his right eye. Tough Tony limped, nature following the art of the imagined St. Valentines Day shooting. Dun led the way, a man with a mission, whatever it was.

"We are a great gang," I said. "There's nothing we can't do." Only my respect for their natural reserve kept me from throwing an arm around each one in kinship. But as we walked, we drifted farther and farther apart. By the time we hit the driveway to the château, we weren't within chatting distance of one another. Each approached the building alone, at his own pace with his own thoughts. Not one light burned from the school to guide us.

Chapter Five

In the cool sweetness of the early hour the Italian maids prepared breakfast with songs and shouts. The scent of strong coffee wafted through the halls. Josh lurked on the balcony like some demented chipmunk gnawing at the French doors of our dorm with his pocketknife. At last he freed the catch, pushed open the doors and shouted, "Up! Up! A new day has dawned!" He swaggered in, hands on hips. His plaid flannel shirt bagged over the belt that held up his shapeless gray-twill trousers. A lock of black hair threatened to cover his dark, deeply set eyes. His upper lip curled in a dismal attempt to convey humor. "What the ruddy hell do you think this is? A bloody Neuchâtel girls' school?" Josh booted the springs of Hermon's cot. The skinny little kid rose to his hands and knees with a groan, his right eye livid and puffed. "Blimey, who popped you?" Josh came close to happy laughter. He spun toward Dun's cot, but seeing the aroused sleeper in his tanktop undershirt, his sun-browned arms at the ready, he shifted to me.

"Ah, yes. The *American.*" He labored for irony, but spouted vinegar. As he tipped my bunk onto its side, I slipped to the floor with the mattress. All this was but a prelude as Josh pounced on Tony's bed with a genuine yelp of pleasure. Grabbing the edge of the springs, he heaved up. Tony, as tall as he was, sailed briefly into the morning, thudded against the wall and slid to rest wedged between bedding and building, still asleep. Miraculously, his pistol hadn't come flying out of his bedclothes.

"Went to the wine festival and tied one on, didn't you?

Now the heads ache and the skin feels like yesterday's newspaper. Well, bad luck for you. Breakfast is now served. Anyone not at table will be given special duties next time a trip to town is contemplated."

"We were just getting up anyway," I said from the floor.

Josh stood in the center of the room, surveyed his male enrollment and wagged his head, supposedly with bemused intolerance for the foibles of youth. But what came from him was nothing less than disgust.

"What happened to your eye?" Wendy asked Hermon at the table.

"He was shanghaied," I explained.

"You can't get shanghaied in Switzerland." Wendy knew that much.

"If you're *from* Shanghai you can be shanghaied anywhere. Two agents saw he was from Shanghai and tried to shanghai him."

"Yeah, and I plugged one in da gut," Tony added.

"Plugged 'em with what, a bathtub stopper?" Wendy giggled at her own joke as she adjusted the front of her blue quilted robe.

"I got the real thing to plug 'em with."

"He's got a trunk full of bathtub stoppers," I butt in. "I'm sure he has one the size of your mouth."

"Ha, ha," she mocked. "Anyway, what country would want to shanghai Hermon? The war is over."

"The war continues in China," Hermon intoned. As usual, his face was a solemn mask, mouth downcast, eyes lowered.

"Yeah," I added. "Haven't you heard of the Communists?"

"Communists are Russians. The Russians aren't fighting the Chinese."

"Tell her, Hermon."

I caught the wink, the setup for one of Hermon's great belches. Like the one he had given during Josh's indoctrination speech. But this time the noise came from the other end, a sweet toot. Then Hermon waved his hands at Wendy as he rattled Shanghai-ese at her.

The four boys lost control, pounding on the table, sputtering and choking with laughter. When I gasped out that Hermon had almost gone to the big teatime in the sky the night before, Tony with a convulsive snort spit out the coffee in his mouth. As though waiting for this display, Josh swept in, halted a few feet from the table and bellowed, "Clean it up! *Maintenant!*"

Tony, erect and rigid, jerking along like an overgrown wooden soldier, disappeared into the kitchen in search of a rag. His flushed face resembled more than ever the maids' special spaghetti sauce with its oregano blemishes, peppered blackheads and diced tomato pimples.

***

I lowered my battered copy of Molière and let my eyes drift across the dimly lit dormitory. Dun waded through the morass of *Dr. Faustus* in German. Hermon picked his toes. Tony rested his head against the wall in his special trance, a hat tilted over his brow. I squeezed shut my eyes then opened them to scan the French dialogue. Suddenly feeling lost and dislocated, I was overcome by loneliness and isolation, a condition I thought I had left behind once the new troops arrived. I wandered down the wide stairs to the library. There in a dark corner nestled the ancient walnut-cased stand-up radio, the kind that in the movies worried Europeans bent over to hear the latest war news. I clicked it on and twirled the dial. The strident voice of the Armed Forces Network broadcasting the World Series engulfed me in solitude.

I missed my father. If I were home, we would be listening to the radio together. Or if he were at work, we would review the game in detail at the first opportunity. Baseball was our bond, our shared obsession. My father had been a good hitting infielder on his high school team. I aimed to equal that, even though the dreaded knowledge ate at me that I never would be.

I missed all the family, especially my mother. She was a trusted friend, someone I could consult on almost any subject. There were feelings I longed to air, although I couldn't pinpoint them. A rambling discourse with my mom would somehow mark a trail to the problem and maybe even to a solution. Even Peggy occupied my thoughts, more than I would have dreamed. I grinned when I remembered how she would blurt out whatever popped into her mind. She overreacted to every social vagary in her class. She filled out a weekly schedule to ensure that I walked the dog as often as she did.

I turned so nostalgic I even contemplated the fortunes of Lily, who had returned to London to recruit more students. For a blind moment I actually missed Lily; her familiar *"Si vous avez fini, vous pouvez partir"* that concluded every meal. The perfume of cigarettes that enveloped her. The light cough that served as a constant in an insecure world.

I closed my eyes and summoned up a fantasy. I dove toward the bag, speared the liner, stepped on third then across the diamond to first. Triple play! That clinched the pennant for the Cubs. They would go into the Series 15-to-1 favorites thanks to my inspired play. I would be the first great athlete to jump from the Big Leagues to the United States Senate. A dazzling leap, yet not improbable considering the man's background. A renowned author of a striking volume of letters written from abroad when he was only 14. An international linguist whose specialties were Swiss French and Molière. A friend of real live

Europeans and Asians. A man who even as a youth recognized massive economic aid to a broken Europe as being in America's best interest. A revolutionary stand for a guy born and raised in America's isolationist breeding ground, Chicago, Illinois. No wonder he was often compared to that great Midwestern internationalist, Senator Arthur Vandenberg of Michigan.

I needed someone to listen to the Series with me. I made my way back upstairs to find Ruthie. Young as she was, maybe nine years old, Ruthie provided company like my little sister Peggy. During the last broadcast she happened by and we started talking.

"Is that baseball?"

"World Series. Dodgers-Yanks. On the Armed Forces Network for the GI's in Europe. If I were home I'd be listening with my father."

"A father who listens to baseball. Jeez." She sat down near me, wet her finger and made a damp design on the little tabletop.

"Doesn't your father like baseball?"

She answered with an expulsion of air at the ridiculous concept.

"What's he do?"

"I don't know. Relief work, I guess. He travels. I never see him."

"Doesn't he know 'Who's on First'?"

"Who *is* on first?" Her eyes brightened as she recognized the routine.

"Who."

"I don't know."

"He's on third."

We broke into laughter. "Why."

"Why?"

"Why's on the team."
"That doesn't sound right."
"Ugga, ugga, boo, ugga boo, boo, ugga."
"Jeez, I forgot that."
"We gotta get serious. There's a big game on here."

Ruthie delivered a perfect copy of Woody Woodpecker, followed by Elmer Fudd: "I'm gonna catch dat cwazy wabbit."

This set us off into more hysterics. She had a great ear and a wicked gleam in her eye. She got the joke, she saw the irony. She was real, like my sister Peggy.

"How did you end up here?" I asked.
"They took me."
"Who?"
"The Brackbirns."
"Who wouldn't take you? You're smart and funny."
"I don't know. All I know is that I'm always going to another school."
"Do you mind that?
"I don't care. They all stink."
"Let's make this one the best one you've ever been to."

Ruthie studied the ceiling.

"We got a good gang here. You're gonna love it."

I heard a rustle outside the library door. I was sure it was Josh about to burst in and ruin everything.

"How about it?" I tried.

Ruthie answered with her best and loudest Woody and we laughed and made cartoon noises. "He's the shortstop," I called lost in the pleasure of being with a person who reminded me of what I had back home.

A figure appeared at the door of the library. Wendy. Ruth clammed up as if apprehended by an authority figure. My laughter died. This was not lost on Wendy, who hurried on without a word.

That had been a few days ago. Now I tapped on their dorm door. "Who's there?" Wendy would have to be the one who answered. She clubbed you to death with her pointless observations. But her forte was the complaining greeting. Like, "Terrible morning we're having, isn't it?" This no matter what the weather and offered in all possible sincerity. Or, "This coffee tastes like liquid mud." I suspected she had the snappiest comebacks in her hometown of Woodmere, Long Island. But we were in Europe, and she was a royal pain in the neck.

"It's Hank. I want to speak to Ruthie."

"It's the middle of the night."

"Ruthie," I called. "Come listen to the World Series. Like we did before."

"She's asleep. Besides, she doesn't care for sports."

"Are you asleep, Ruth?"

"I told you she was. Would I lie?"

Instead of rekindling the campfire of companionship with Ruthie, I heard Wendy's querulous voice: "Why do they broadcast the World Series over here? The Europeans don't care about baseball. Maybe they're broadcasting to the Chinese while they fight the Communists." Her skeptical laughter fell like broken crystal on the stairway.

I sank into the leather chair and fell into a deep Tough Tony–style trance. Gionfriddo's historic catch that robbed DiMaggio of a homer drifted through my consciousness without leaving a ripple.

A huge form loomed in the portal, two-headed and bulky. I rose unsteadily to my feet. Josh and his mother blocked the doorway, their arms around each other's waist. I edged toward them and mumbled to Lily, "Welcome back." She didn't respond. They stared at me as though I were prowling their bedroom. They smelled of the festival—white wine and the autumn night.

When I passed close enough to touch them, Josh moved and I slipped by. At the landing I glanced back. They tracked me, their arms still around each other.

※※※

"Have you heard about the French chaps?" Dun asked me.
"What French chaps?"
We sprawled on the stone wall of the terrace at midmorning break. Monsieur Montraux had just putted off on his silver BSA motorcycle after leaving the mail. The peaks of Switzerland sparkled before us, clearer and sharper than the day I arrived with Josh. The great sweep of the lush country rose to cradle the Sea of Clouds, the billowy vapor undulating in its confines. Perched on the shore of this ethereal reach we saw the roll of the land and the frosted massive rise of the Alps—especially the Jungfrau group—as they emerged in the distance. In this way, the sea both obscured and revealed. I could never observe this expanse dispassionately, even on a fresh, crisp day that promised no dark surprises. The mist always seemed inhabited by unseen spirits that could somehow rise up to affect our lives.

"We're to get four French chaps as students," Dun said. "None can speak English. That should help your French."

"French guys? I thought Lily had been in London."

"Among other places." Dun gripped a knee and rocked on his haunches. He bore the air of a man who knew things. Dun didn't speculate.

Josh crept up behind us and shook his hand bell sharply in our ears. As we shied away from the noise, the headmaster contorted his sardonic half-smile. "English literature," he said. He made it sound like a jail sentence.

Josh called his entire student body foreigners. One of his favorite expressions: "It's too complicated for you foreigners to understand." This facilitated his escape when at a loss to explain some point of English grammar or social history. He intended a jest, but he couldn't delete the dash of venom in his delivery. In the strictest sense some of us were foreigners. Wendy, Ruth and I were Americans. Hermon came from the missionary schools of China. Although an Englishman like Josh, Dun resembled a French Resistance fighter, thus a quasi foreigner. But Tony, an Englishman to the core, could never be classified as a foreigner. His pale horse face, broad accent and casual slouch that bordered on physical impairment cast him as a fair-complected cousin of Josh. If anything, he was too much like Josh for the headmaster's taste.

"You foreigners are destroying English letters!"

Josh scooped up the book of great English literature from in front of Tony, who had been reading aloud. Tony's monotone, clogged vowels and air of desperate boredom had us all nodding and drooping. Josh paced to the glass doors, gazed across the Sea of Clouds, wheeled and rendered *Sir Gawain and the Green Knight* as he imagined the King would have intended.

The arm not holding the book flailed in the still classroom air. Spittle flew in sparkling showers. His black hair danced on his bobbing head, his eyelids negligible slits as he read his lines.

He lifts his axe lightly, and lets it down deftly,
The blade's edge next to his naked neck.
Though mightily hammered he hurt him no more
Than to give him a slight nick that severed the skin there.

Suddenly he raised his arms as though silencing an angry crowd and proclaimed into the void, "Explain that, sir!" The room remained hushed, no one certain whom Josh was addressing. "I said, 'Explain that, sir!'" Josh's face turned the color of a strawberry as he gestured toward Tony.

"Do you mean me?" Tony's voice squeaked small and hesitant.

"Yes, I mean you."

"Explain what?"

Josh hurled the volume of great English literature at Tony's head. It slammed into the wall beside his temple and fell broken to the floor. "You clod!" Josh shrieked. "Destroy yourself if you will. But do not profane great literature with your bloody inattention."

Tony sat in place. His pink-rimmed eyes blinked at the spot on the table where the book had rested, his face impassive. Only the clasping and unclasping of his long fingers signaled his awareness. Without warning a wave of passionate heat engulfed me as all my rebellious feelings welled up. I struggled to contain myself. Tony should rise up and fight back. I burned ready to join him. This stupid school. Josh and his unpredictable mood swings. Attacking us in our beds. His pathetic classroom routines. He wasn't teaching us, but showing off in front of a bunch of trapped kids. How much of this could we take? But Tony remained in his chair.

Josh silently retrieved the book, found his place and resumed his performance. He drew in a breath, exhaled toward the god of English literature and continued:

Pulled out his bright sword, and said in a passion
(And since he was mortal man born of his mother
the hero was never so happy by half . . .

The nasal voice of Josh whined like a buzz saw rising and falling with the strain of hitting knots of wood. The boy-man tottered first on one foot, then the other, his head whipping from side to side as though hooked on a windshield wiper.

And care!
Here I confess my sin;
And faulty did I fare.
Your goodwill let me win,

and then I will beware.

Cottony foam at the corners of his mouth, he bowed his head to accept applause. In the quiet, we boys struggled to avoid each other's eyes. Josh was a joke, but we couldn't laugh at him. I clenched, waiting for Hermon to belch, or worse. Our jaws tightened, fingers clutching pencils until I expected to hear them snap. Someone had to say or do something to break the tension, or we all would explode. Then from Tony's corner of the table came a resonant English, "Ho, ho, ho."

Josh's face, benign in triumph, ignited with hate as the sun-porch classroom filled with relieved laughter. Everyone let go, even Wendy, who was usually the most obedient. Stunned and confused by this odd rebellion, Josh lowered his book and approached Tony. As suddenly as the laughter had erupted, it was muffled. In quiet fury, Josh stretched out his trembling hands, his target Tony's neck. But instead of attacking, he raised a bony finger toward the door and said, "Get out of this room and don't you *ever* come back."

Tony fought to regain passivity, but Josh's reading had swept away his reserve. As he collected his notebook and pencil, a remaining guffaw escaped. Josh lunged toward him, and, without thinking, I jumped between them. Josh and I exchanged bitter glances for some long moments while the student body gaped in wonder. The lunch bell defused the confrontation. We kids broke from Josh's little kingdom like prisoners rushing through a breached wall.

Chapter Six

The burning wood in the water heater crackled, the pungent smoke autumn incense. The coursing hot water soothed as well as cleansed, a weekly treat for body and soul. Somehow, Thursday night became ordained for showers. We boys built the fire, and when the water warmed, Josh went, then Lily. The girls followed, then us. Between shifts, we fed the flames with split logs not much larger then kindling. When it finally came our turn, we luxuriated in the rush of hot water. The spacious tile bathroom filled with steam as Dun and Hermon shared one of the marble stalls and Tony and I the other.

Engrossed with soaping my loins, I checked for the thousandth time the slow progress there. Again I agonized: What was taking me so long to arrive at manhood? The process had begun, but sexual maturity seemed as distant as ever. In my most secure moments I convinced myself of my soundness; minor physical release crowned my erotic rapture. But at weaker times, the wondering bedeviled me. Was I to be some kind of half-ready mutant? It preoccupied me because every other boy my age seemed to have come to physical sexual fruition, including Tony, who stood naked beside me.

An odd sound like water running off a roof drew me from my speculation. Tony wore a platter-shaped rain hat, the water gushing off it.

"Why are you wearing your hat in the shower?"

"Am I?' Tony reached up and felt the hat. "So I am. I thought I was riding in my Jag convertible in the rain."

We four dried ourselves slowly in the tiled room.

"You have a Jag?" I asked.

"An ancient one. Like a gangster car, in point of fact. My mother has two cars." The attention made Tony expansive. "She has her order in for a new Jag."

"What does your father do?" Tony never mentioned him.

"Do?"

"His job."

Tony adopted his blank stare, nonplussed by the enormity of the question. I changed tack. "Why are you in this crazy school if your mother's rich?"

"We all have rich families," Tony tried.

"My father's a newspaperman. Only publishers get rich on newspapers."

"Fewer are rich in England now," Dun intoned as steady as ever. "Levels the playing field. All for the best."

"My father showed me a teletype from London that said English money couldn't leave the country."

"Five pounds only," Dun said. "Even for vacation trips."

"How can anyone pay for school in Switzerland?"

"Princess Elizabeth is taking care of that," Dun said with a straight face. "She's not buying a new trousseau for her wedding to Philip."

"That should do it," Tony said.

"Problem solved," Hermon added.

"How do the Brackbirns pay for things?" I persisted even as I wondered how my school chums got their tuition money.

"There are places that keep money for you," Dun said.

"Like Switzerland," I said.

"That's it," Tony said. "They have their money in Swiss banks."

"In numbered accounts," Hermon chimed. "Like gangsters and playboys."

"How do you know about things like that, Hermon?" I asked.

"I know about money and cheating. That's how I got here."

The others found this very amusing, and I laughed along. But I wasn't sure if he was kidding, serious or repeating gossip from the British tabloids.

"Money is private business," I assured them in my best Midwest booster tone, eager to restore solidarity. "Remember, the other night we did something no man has ever done before in the history of recorded time." I eyed them, seeking the confirming nod or gesture. But each remained unresponsive. "Come on. Don't deny what we did."

"We shan't forget." Dun's smile brought the others around.

"Unparalleled in history."

"Death-defying."

"An act to be told future generations."

"Today," I added, "Tough Tony stood up to Sir Gawain and brought him to his knees."

"Smote him rather cleanly," Hermon echoed.

Tony tucked his towel around his waist and slowly became Josh. He hunched his shoulders until they were bony folded wings. His eyelids closed, then fluttered, struggling to rise yet lacking the interest to make it. His head hung like an overripe apple too tenacious to fall, and his lower lip dipped.

"You foreigners are destroying English letters." His inflection echoed Josh. He became Josh's idiot cousin. "Destroy yourselves, if you will, but do not profane great literature. I shall not tolerate it in this eminent hall of learning. Not at the Swiss English *Bombing* Academy." His voice rattled the windows. Tony's fiendish cackle raked laughter and cheers from his cohorts.

Josh stood in the middle of the dorm, legs apart, running the blade of his pocketknife under a thumbnail. If he had heard Tony's shower-room show, he gave no intimation. The boys stepped around him as though skirting a piece of furniture and crawled onto their cots.

"We should like to see you all downstairs." His expression, stance and intonation made him seem a pale imitation of Tony doing Josh. Somehow Tony did Josh better than Josh did himself. "Now!" Josh barked. In pj's and bare feet we padded down the stairway to the little library, its stale air thick with smoke from Josh's and Lily's cigarettes.

"This meeting," Josh began, "is to commemorate your final day in this school." His voice trembled with excitement. "You are all expelled."

Bounced from this madhouse on a mountain. That was the answer to everything. I fought not to smile, yet the pleasure of relief was so profound, I feared bursting into tears. Leaving Josh and Lily at last with their pitiful games aimed at controlling and lording it over kids. No style. No class. Not European at all. Not what I expected when I left home. Kiss it goodbye, return to the States where life was real. Still, as the flush of excitement faded, a subtle distress gripped me. I was committed to sticking it out for myself, my family, the gang at Hillard School and the honor of America. We hadn't won the war by quitting. Now Josh and Lily Brackbirn were cheating me out of that.

"None of you are stricken with grief. So much the better." But Josh couldn't mask his disappointment. "We feel no need to justify this move. But for the sake of your memory books, we shall provide some reasons." He aimed a long arm at me, his head down. "The *American*." The repulsion with which he said the word wrenched his face. "Our grandest disappointment. Full scholarship. The choice of a supposedly distinguished private school..."

"Not supposedly. You know it's the best."

"Kindly hold your insolent tongue." Josh snuffled in the contents of his nose and gagged it down with some difficulty. "He speaks English at table. Makes sarcastic jokes during class instead of studying. He *chains* himself to the radio without permission to listen to the babble of an *American* sports announcer."

"You once invited me to listen."

"Silence!" Josh cut off my rebuttal with a chop of his hand, then directed his ire at Hermon. "Our young Chinese friend is frivolous and crude. Anyone who has heard his effusions will scarcely question that." Facing Dun, he struggled. "This one is after something not available here."

Like what? Dun of all people assumed the role of dispassionate observer. The calm, strong one whose reach never exceeded his grasp. Typical of Josh to miss the point on Dun.

The boy-headmaster paused for a moment, savoring his final assault. In repose he gained a boyish air, an alert undergraduate with a congenial willingness to learn. He's like a student, I thought. Maybe 19 or 20. And Lily, 40 at most. In a moment of crisis like this I took pride in my ability to survey the scene, catch details. Good training if I ever hoped to be a good newsman like my father. Josh built his enthusiasm, savoring the prospect of laying waste Anthony Joseph Heath-Merriweather. When he spoke, his voice trilled with the thrill of the kill. "As for this one. He is surely our rottenest apple."

A pang of jealousy. Surely I ranked as the rottenest apple. By the weight of seniority alone, I deserved the title.

"He is arrogant, lazy, slovenly and slow. His hygiene is deplorable, and in class he besmirches the literary achievements of the greatest culture the world has ever produced. I could continue but hardly feel the subject worth my intellect."

As Josh paused for the boys to simmer in shame, he assumed the stance of persecuted prophet, arms raised, hands dangling, awaiting the nails and cross. Hermon covered his mouth with a hand as if to belch. We all clenched, but Tony didn't clench hard enough. His snort of laughter shook the little library.

From his martyr's pose Josh spoke in clipped disdain. "Leave ... this room ... and pack your bloody trunk ... before I commit mayhem!"

Tony hurried out, his long toenails ticking on the wooden floor. I had never heard human toenails click on a floor before.

"The rest of you, stay here."

"Wait, dear." Lily's voice broke brittle in the cool room.

"No, Mother. I know what I'm about."

"You're excited, dear."

"As for the rest of you." He tried to sound chummy. But his counterfeit friendliness offended more than his genuine anger. "That chap ... "

"Dear!" Her cold tone drove an icicle into his speech.

"Get out! All of you."

As we broke for the door, Josh retreated to his mother. Lily opened her arms as her son hunched up, shrinking himself to a size small enough to be accepted on the inviting breast that swelled under her sweater.

Tony smoothed out his bell-bottoms, the cuffs under his chin. He still wore his striped flannel pajama bottoms with a wrinkled dress shirt.

"Don't pack," I ordered. "None of us are going anywhere."

"I am," Tony said.

"Not unless we give the okay. If we hang together, we can all stay."

"But we've been cashiered," Hermon protested.

"We haven't been cashiered," I assured, not certain what

that word meant. "They're bluffing. That's what Josh was about to tell us when Lily stopped him. We can stay if we let Tony go."

"But you chaps didn't have me tossed out." Tony didn't get it.

"Here's the way I see it." This is where I exuded confidence—the clinching argument. Why America should support the United Nations and not try to run the world by itself. Why it was insane to consider dropping the atomic bomb on Russia now to get it over with, as many readers of the *Chicago Tribune* believed. "For some reason Josh would like to throw Tony out. But he needs our permission to do it. We're supposed to write to our friends about what a great place this is. Get them to enroll. That's why he offered a scholarship to my school."

"I get it, ya mug," Tony tried his gangster jargon in an effort to sound convinced.

"We don't have any rich friends," Hermon said.

"But to throw us out would close the school," I countered.

"What about the four French chaps?" Hermon asked.

"Don't hold your breath till you see them," I said. "Look, I spent days alone here waiting for students who never came. I didn't have to be Einstein to realize I was the school. Lose me and they lose the student body. It's the same now if the four of us stick together." I fell back on my bed, wallowing in my American-bred certitude. The others gave no sign of being won over. In fact, they seemed downright perplexed.

"The headmaster needs our permission to throw Tony out." Hermon stumbled on this concept.

"Wait and see." I shot a look at Dun. He was the key person, the one to be swayed. But Dun remained an enigma in cool detachment. My doubts edged in. "Just in case, let's exchange addresses."

Without comment, we printed our names and mailing addresses in the school notebooks. I scribbled:

Hank Douglas
26 Scott Street
Chicago, Illinois
USA
North American Continent
Western Hemisphere
World
Solar System
Universe

"Let's never forget," I intoned, "the night the four of us did something no man has ever done before."

The nods and grunts assured me they remained aware of the event. But the reaction was tentative. It lacked the bold camaraderie of earlier in the evening after our showers.

※※※

"It's Tuesday, not Sunday. Why are you all dressed up?" Wendy was unaware of the previous night's action.

"We've been cashiered," Tony said.

"We're going home," Hermon added.

"Liars," Wendy concluded with a big smile.

Josh and Lily emerged from the library, cigarette smoke heavy behind them, the flush of conspiracy in their cheeks. Perfect mates, they could have boarded the ark arm in arm. Josh swung his leg over the back of the chair, dropped into it and plopped his elbows on the table.

"The four *boys*. In the study. After breakfast. *Du lait, s'il vous plaît.*"

In the library, Josh spoke with a weariness that surpassed his usual English intellectual's boredom. "Mrs. Brackbirn and I spent a long and troubled night agonizing over the wisest course regarding you four." The sorrow dragged down his body. "At least with three of you ... "

I braced to spring. We all stay or we all leave. Dun winked at me in support. Convinced we'd win, I braced for battle.

"We have reached the conclusion that *all* of you deserve another chance."

All? Again I felt cheated by the authorities, the conflict denied me, sure victory withdrawn.

Josh spoke toward Tony. "At least in one case, we arrive at this decision with great reluctance. But we feel, in the best interest of the school, to give it one more try with all you chaps." Josh's voice grew light, his countenance open. He could be companionable, even likable, which made his behavior all the more tough to take. Being a jerk was a choice, not a genetic curse.

"*All* of us?" My confrontational tone spoiled the mood of reconciliation.

"You heard my statement," Josh snapped.

But before the familiar hard stances could be resumed, Tony sang out, "Good show!" It was so proper and fitting and English that we all laughed, even the Brackbirns.

"May I add a word?" I couldn't let it go with a bland smile. Josh eyed his mother, who made no objection. I started, keeping my approach diplomatic. "I can say for my part that I'm very happy you decided to keep us. But the recent bad feelings aren't caused by us boys alone. A lot's gone wrong that was beyond our control. We have a small school, smaller than any of us expected. But we know what the money situation is in England and Europe. Still, I don't think the administration should take it out on us because they don't have many students.

"We all want a big and prosperous school, and we are

willing to work toward that end. But for the school to grow, the students must feel that the administration is with them, not against them."

I leaned back against the wall, boiling inside my tweed suit. My jacket bound my arms and the trousers chafed. The room fell still.

"Well," Josh boomed, not sure if he had been put down or backed up. "That helps clear the air. Not that I condone criticism of our school. But let's make this a new beginning in the spirit of the library. A fresh start ... "

"We shall all get along much better from now on," Lily interrupted. "Go to your rooms now and prepare for your morning lessons." She always made the château sound like an elite university where each student had a suite of rooms and a man to lay out proper clothing. Her voice cut like a gust of winter wind, her face as changeable as the Swiss mountain weather.

We ran up to the dorm and slammed the door. Tony jumped onto his bed, clenched his hands together and shook them first near his left ear, then near his right, like a prizefighter in a movie.

"They knew we were united," I shouted. "They sensed it and gave in."

In triumph I liked Tony so much, liked them all so much, I let out a whoop. I pounded little Hermon on the back and shook Dun's fleshy paw. Tony ripped off my bedclothes and threw them over his head. With the sheet draped over him, he was nothing less than the ghost of the present. I hurled myself at the wraith that was Tony, and Hermon followed. Dun watched, shaking his head like an indulgent parent. The class bell caught us. We ran downstairs streaming with sweat in our travel clothes.

Chapter Seven

The sense of power started as a warm flow that built into a fever that inflamed me. Following the confrontation in the library, I knew I could foil Josh's snares and ambushes. I was a force in the school. Before, when I blurted out to my friends that my scholarship was a lure to bring my richer classmates over from Chicago, I had stated a simple truth. Of course Josh counted on my returning home with glowing tales of life abroad. Expelling his scholarship boy would hardly elevate his tiny institution. Tossing the scholarship boy's buddy would also have negative repercussions. Josh and I engaged in a cold war, with my client, Tony, in the middle.

On the terrace at mail time Josh deliberately collided with Tony. He brushed by him, threw an elbow into his ribs and then hurried on without a word. These sneak attacks were repeated randomly, but Tony showed no annoyance with the aggression.

"Don't let him get to you, Tough Tony," I confided. "We're with youse."

Tony raised his blond eyebrows and surveyed the Sea of Clouds.

One afternoon, I arrived at the dining room for tea to see Tony trapped in a corner by Josh, who circled his hands with menace near Tony's head, the spray of spittle flying into the boy's face. I stepped up, about to remind Josh that he was violating the spirit of the library. But Josh broke off, leaving Tony propped in the corner like an upside-down dust mop.

"Tell us if he bothers you too much," I demanded.

"No one bothers Tough Tony."

Later that afternoon, Wendy and Tony were sitting on the terrace, Tony's face the customary mask of imperturbability. Wendy sparked their chat, her fingers caressing the air like butterflies. They alighted on Tony's arm and patted him in reassurance.

"Any letters today?" Hermon asked me.

"One from my sister."

"Wizard! Of course we shall have a reading."

Since his arrival, Hermon had been enthralled by the snippets of news and gossip contained in my family's letters from Chicago, which I often read aloud. Now he insisted that every letter be shared. He even devised a special position for my recitations. He rested his head in the middle of his bed with his legs extended up the wall. If he didn't hear something, or didn't quite grasp its meaning, he insisted I read it again, and, if necessary, explain it. The sessions became an informal classroom on postwar Chicago life. Dun and Tony, although they never agitated for readings, didn't depart when I began one.

"There was a fuss in the *Tribune*," Peggy wrote. "For an assembly on national anthems of the world we sang the 'Internationale.' The *Tribune* had a fit. By singing the anthem of the Soviet Union, the school showed its true colors, deep pink. They actually wrote that in an editorial. Those people are crazy."

"The *Tribune* thinks we're a Commie school," I explained to the others, who were lying on their cots waiting for the supper bell. "That's because we believe in the U.N. We think the Negroes are still practically slaves in the South. And the Nisei, the Japanese-Americans, were shafted but good during the war by being dumped into concentration camps. A kid who grew up in a camp is in my class. He told us everything."

Peggy talked about the tryouts for the class play: "Bob Davis is the best actor, but the lead went to Leonard Circo. If they always rewarded the best actor with the lead, Bob Davis would win every time."

"At Hillard everyone gets a chance," I explained. "Otherwise the best people would dominate. Everyone goes out for sports, everyone gets to play. Unless we have a chance to win, especially against Boys' Latin." Even on a Swiss mountain it made sense to me.

"Dick Cohen threw an open house while his parents were out of town," Peggy wrote. "This was the first time we eighth-graders held our own party without chaperons. Everyone danced with the lights out in that *gigantic* apartment on Lake Shore Drive. There were stars in my eyes for *days* afterward. Now we call Dick the King Farouk of the North Side."

I read the last few lines to myself. Peggy missed me. Dog missed me. The kids at school asked about me "constantly." When I returned, she expected me to teach her French, or at the very least do her French homework.

"Read that part about dancing with the lights out again," Hermon demanded. I obeyed, but when Hermon cried out, "Jolly good!" and drummed his heels against the wall in excitement, I faced a moment of real doubt about sharing my private correspondence.

"I read my mail to you, Hermon. It's your turn to read me yours."

"I don't get mail."

"Sure you do."

"Form letters from my guardian. They would put you to sleep."

"Tell me about missionary school."

"Little to tell."

"You learned English there."

Hermon remained silent.

"Where's your family now?" I asked.

"Safe."

"Where?"

Hermon would never reveal his family background and he quickly changed the subject. "How old is your sister?"

"Twelve."

"Exactly my age. Good-o!"

"Barely twelve," I added quickly. "If you're interested in my sister, I have to know more about you," I tried the mock-serious approach.

"Time enough for that," Hermon responded, sounding far more the man of the world than I.

Josh suggested a school Ping-Pong tournament after supper. At least that's what we thought he said. Josh mumbled to cover his shaky command of French, but the words Ping-Pong rose from the nasal tones.

"Look lively, can't chat all night." Josh slapped Dun on the shoulder in his false hail-fellow way, breaking the quiet French conversation the student was pursuing with Lily. Josh ordered us to clear off the classroom table on the sun porch while he dragged the folding Ping-Pong tabletop from a corner. As he prepared the tournament chart, the student body gathered round him more engrossed than we ever were in studies.

Josh played a free-swinging game, but in his match with Wendy she slowed him down by setting her own rules.

"That wasn't out," she declared after one of her shots. "It ticked the edge of the table. Didn't you hear it?"

Josh's jaw went slack, his paddle dangling from his hand.

"I heard it. My point."

After one of Josh's service aces she whined, "No fair. I

wasn't ready. Take it again." To my astonishment he bowed to her every demand and even tried his version of a smile after one of her lame excuses. Still he won, although it took him twice as long as it normally would have.

Josh vs. Dun seemed a match played by madmen. They smashed the ball with abandon, often ignoring the table between them. I never saw Dun so wild, a secret anger unchained. Josh responded in kind, crashing the ball directly at Dun with little regard for the playing surface or the point. What was going on between those two? At that point I couldn't see the obvious.

Then Josh cleverly shifted tactics. While Dun continued the slashing game, Josh placed soft returns for winning points. At the end he was toying with the younger player. With the game won, Josh shot an elated look at his mother, who watched from the doorway, her arms folded, her expression as peaceful as a dawn after a storm.

I beat Hermon and Tony with steadiness and refused to be suckered into Josh's reckless game. In frustration, Josh grew more and more aggressive, finally giving up the last point by sending the ball careering into a porch window. After Josh lost, he skimmed his paddle across the tabletop. It skittered under the net and glanced off my leg. "This is your night. There shall be others." He stormed from the room to burst into the library where his mother awaited, presumably to curl up on her lap. "Don't forget." Josh materialized in the doorway. "A quiz on *King Lear* in the morning."

Wendy groaned. Josh had mentioned nothing of *King Lear* all day. "That's not fair," she scolded. "We can't read all of *King Lear* tonight."

Josh's face clouded as he intoned something about foreigners. Then he added, "We shall see, shan't we?" The library door closed behind him.

"Are you going to read *King Lear* tonight?" she asked me.

"I already know it by heart."

"You don't even know who wrote it."

"Marlowe. He wrote all of Shakespeare's stuff."

"Come on, Ruth. We're going to read *King Lear*. All we can anyway. If we flunk the test, let him lump it."

Dun suggested a few turns around the house. He began at his customary brisk pace then broke into a trot, and soon he and I were running around and around the château. The crisp, clean night air pierced the nostrils and scoured the lungs. From out of nowhere Pancho appeared and now loped at our side. Even though I defended the setter against Josh's temperamental kicks, Pancho paid little heed to anyone save his master. That Pancho bestirred himself to run marked another good omen in this night of small victories.

When we snapped on the dormitory ceiling light, Hermon moaned and pulled the covers over his head. Tony's rumpled bed gaped empty.

"Where's Tony?"

"Leave the chap alone," Dun commanded as he doused the light.

"We should find him before Josh does."

Dun huffed as he undressed in the dark. If we were walking, he would have sped his pace to a trot; that was his response to unwanted discussions. But I was determined. I produced my flashlight and set out in search of Tony.

I checked the kitchen and dining room. In the sun-porch classroom my light picked out the net across the table. A swirl of self-satisfaction comforted me as I recalled how I had dispatched Josh. I may be slow at French and tardy in becoming a physical man, but I could play Ping-Pong better than anyone in the school.

The library door creaked open, my light dancing across the empty room. No one by the radio. The closet contained only coats. In the kitchen, I eased open the door and played the light down the cellar stairs.

"Tony? You down there?" my whispers deadened by the cavity.

I stood outside the girls' bedroom. If I opened the door and Josh caught me, I'd be headed back to Chicago on the first boat, scholarship kid or not. I'd sound lame explaining to the Hillard student body how I had been bounced for sneaking into the girls' dorm while searching for my buddy. Rather than barge in like a brash American, I slipped in with stealth like a European. I shone my light across the floor until it reached the foot of Wendy's bed. I wondered whether the beam would find those long toes with the unclipped nails that ticked on wooden floors. If it did, what would I do? What made me conjure up such a preposterous scene?

Wendy's terrified eyes glowed in the weak gleam. I clicked off the light and stole out the door, closing it softly. Back in the boys' dorm Tony's bed remained vacant. A cigarette ember glowed from Dun. A cold claw of abandonment clutched my heart. I stood alone in a foreign world, my friends unreachable, my knowledge of them minimal despite my efforts. I tried. I opened up my life, but they kept theirs a secret that made me feel uninvited. When I thought I understood them, they slipped away. I was alone following instincts I wasn't sure I understood. Somehow the struggle to control Tony rose as a purpose of the trip abroad. But why, and what to do about it, left me confused and rattled.

In the bathroom relieving myself I repeated my entreaty: Please hurry. Make me a man. Then I'll know what I'm supposed to do. Tired of worrying about the school and everyone in it, I craved the escape of sleep. Outside in the hall, Wendy's figure brought me up.

"Were you just in our room?" she demanded.

"I was looking for Tough Tony."

"In our room?"

"I can't find him."

"Why are you after him?"

"I'm afraid he's going to get into trouble."

"I think you're the one looking for trouble."

"In your room?" I flashed my most incredulous smile.

We whispered loudly, like children who wish to be heard. Then as if focused by the twist of a telescope, a tall door made itself clear behind Wendy. The linen closet. I moved her aside and opened the door. The flashlight ray caught the bare ankles. His pajama-clad legs curled against his body, knees against chest, right thumb in mouth. As we watched, Tony took a long suck on his thumb and nestled deeper into the pile of dirty sheets.

Feeling a traitor for exposing my buddy in a vulnerable state to a girl, I quickly closed the door. A cold draft chilled the hallway. Reflexively for warmth, I slipped my arm around Wendy's shoulder, my hand experiencing the softness of her quilted robe, so familiar from breakfast. Her hand moved around my waist and she turned with face uplifted. I found her lips tight but warm.

The curve of her hip pressed against me and I moved against it. My tongue slipped between her lips. Her hand stroked the back of my neck. She was tender, supple. It didn't take long for the tingling to shudder through my body.

"It was cold here alone," I said, my voice heavy, still a bit dazed by what had just happened.

"It's all right. Honey." She sounded like a wife reassuring her mate of many years, echoing her mother's voice to her father.

She kissed me again with frozen innocence and whispered, "My darling."

Only then did I remember this was Wendy, the pain in the neck who whined through life and never got the drift. I must make clear immediately that a terrible mistake had occurred. This was Wendy, for God's sake. I had to ditch her before someone saw.

But when she cuddled my hand in hers, an odd current raced between us. Even in my frantic state of denial, I couldn't slough off this physical reality. She squeezed my hand, rested her head against my arm, then let go and disappeared down the hall.

"Tony's sleeping in the dirty sheets," I said toward Dun's bed.

"Is that so?"

"Suppose Josh finds him there?"

Dun grunted. I pulled off my trousers. I smelled dead flowers, the dampness a cold spot at my loins.

Chapter Eight

A light rain sifted through the mist to beat a gentle tattoo on the dying leaves as our boots slapped the road to town. Dun and I left Hermon in the kitchen teaching the two Italian maids to say in English, "It's foggy today." Some of the educational zeal of the missionary school remained with Hermon after all.

Dun had been even more uncommunicative than usual lately. I feared that my intrusion into Tony's life the night before had upset him. I assured Dun that my concern was strictly for Tough Tony's welfare. Dun gave little response, and I strove harder to reach him by reviewing familiar territory, stuff we had covered when we first met and took those long walks in the woods to escape the Swiss English Academy.

"How did you get the name Dun?"

"It was my version of David. The world followed."

"At your other schools could you walk to town like this?"

"*Mais oui*," delivered in a mildly mocking tone.

We clipped down the mountain road, Dun setting his usual quick pace. A sturdy fellow, sinewy and tanned, he was not handsome. His angular face tilted slightly off center, and his large eyes protruded like a nocturnal predator's. But the stillness at his core dispensed strength. He was older than I, about Tony's age, but Tony was a boy next to Dun. I pushed Dun to recount his childhood again, how he had lived in Paris and learned perfect French. But Dun waved this off as old news. I remembered when he arrived at the school and we sat in the clearing in the woods.

"My father was in business in Paris. I was born there. My mother and I left in 1940. My father escaped the Nazis at Dunkirk."

"Dunkirk?"

"He had volunteered for the British Army in France. He came back from the Continent on a fishing boat."

"He escaped from Dunkirk in a fishing boat?"

"Many did," Dun assured me that afternoon.

"Hell, I know that," I squawked. "I saw *Mrs. Miniver*."

"Did you, now?" Dun zipped up his leather jacket as he rose. "Teatime." He set off toward the school. I hurried to keep pace.

But that had been weeks earlier, when I was a kid, a naïve American. Now I was more experienced. I kept after Dun as we hiked, urging him to relate more of his background, to divulge his secrets. "You really went at Josh in Ping-Pong last night."

"Small profit for me."

"You lost, but you really let him have it." I waited to allow Dun to detail his gripe with Josh. No response. "Josh can be a real pain." Another pause for confirmation, which wasn't made. "He claims to want harmony, but he's picking on us all the time."

"It's his school." His delivery exceeded neutrality, it reeked of fatalism. Dun picked up the pace with a perfunctory grunt. We fell into a forced silence marked only by rapid footfalls and measured breathing.

No sweeping plain spread before Neuchâtel inviting the visitor to contemplate its medieval heritage and charm. Instead, we hikers stumbled on it as we plunged down the Jura hills. The Brackbirns' old guidebook gave a florid description of the town:

Crawling up the steep slopes from its nesting place by the

lake, the turreted town remains a remnant from the age of the longbow and heavily embroidered myths. Almost a thousand years ago the private preserve of an aristocratic French family, the town eventually passed into the possession of the King of Prussia. Then Napoleon had his turn, and after some typical European political skirmishes and intrigues it became a canton in the Swiss Federation. Through it all, Neuchâtel held a position as a great intellectual center with a renowned university and a pure tongue considered the finest French in Switzerland.

That was the town the tourists were supposed to see. What we saw that afternoon was a smear of blue autumnal haze mingled with the whiff of roasting chestnuts. The bells of the tram rang sharply. Men wore winter hob-nailed boots in readiness for the inevitable snow, their heels snapping on the narrow cobblestone streets. Their faces were flushed and ruddy as they broke from the stores and bistros whose windows were steamed over.

Dun and I toured the town, halting only to duck into the small shops so I could practice my French with pointless questions directed at the clerks, many of whom were tolerant if not talkative. We walked without purpose, past the 15th-century castle and prison that reared up as the defensive heart of the fortress city and had served as the residence of the many counts of Neuchâtel. We ambled along the city's cramped streets that bloomed with colorful fountains and bustling restaurants and cafés. Many of the buff-hued stone buildings had towers, steep gabled roofs and walls inset with tile. In these tight confines I noted the contrast with my native Chicago, which was also by a lake. But Chicago spilled outward, its limitless expanses of beaches edging an endless Lake Michigan. This Swiss haven huddled by the water before crawling up the hills.

The basketball court by the lake cultivated tufts of

crabgrass the size of a man's head. A few boys played their own game of kicking the ball from one basket to the other, then picking it up and shooting it at the hoop. Soccer-basketball, Swiss style. A swirl of wind carried a curl of clay dust across the court, causing one of the backboards to creak. The beach was nearly deserted. A few couples strolled while some children and a dog ran near the water. Several sailboats bobbed and dipped among the whitecaps.

Sitting on the sand, staring across Lake Neuchâtel toward the Alps with Mont Blanc poking through the clouds, Dun spoke in French. He recited something about a brother in France at the beginning of the war. His language lilted in Parisian purity, its cadence rising and falling hypnotically. Desperate for any scrap of his personal history, I clamped onto his words, crouched forward, face furrowed with effort. But as often happened, I became enraptured by the sounds and lost the thread of the narrative. The act of listening consumed me, comprehension a casualty.

The story stirred emotion in Dun. Tears formed in the older boy's eyes as I struggled to understand. In sheer frustration, I pleaded with him to speak more slowly. The request shattered the mood, making him aware of himself, his listener and the setting. He chuckled and said in English, "It's foggy today." He stood, brushed the sand from his gray tweed knickers and pronounced, "We shall miss supper."

The slopes began their rise well before we broke from the confines of the little city. As we marched under the skeletal branches that arched over the road, Dun began again in French. Struggling to match him step for step, I strained to catch his words. Difficult on the beach in repose, the one-way conversation was further shackled by walking and Dun's lowered voice. To keep Dun revved, I repeated at regular intervals, *"Je comprends."*

But my head echoed with the foreign sounds and the pain of faked understanding.

These words bobbed up from the flow of French: "Paris. Dunkirk. Nazis. Refugees." Then came a quiet altering of the voice and the name, "Lily." What about Lily? What did Dun know? But I didn't dare request clarification, or Dun would clam up.

Halfway up, we sat on an outcropping of rock and smoked. Without fanfare, Dun concluded his story in French. In the aftermath, the young man fixed his gaze straight ahead, not intimating that he sought a reaction. He had been talking to himself and I knew it, spilling out a secret to a deaf and dumb companion who desired nothing more than to be a confidant.

***

At lunch Josh wouldn't pass Tony the milk. Twice Tony asked for the pitcher in French but it remained at Josh's elbow. Tony sat staring at his empty glass until I stood, grabbed the pitcher, walked to Tony's place and poured. I sat and resumed eating while the entire table pretended not to have noticed. The war of wills between Josh and me over Tony raged on.

As we departed the table, we heard Pancho's brief yelp, then Josh snapped with irritation, "I say, Pancho, must you forever be underfoot?" But when Wendy cooed her concern for the dog, Josh came full circle. "Sorry, boy. There's a good fellow." He gave the animal a perfunctory tickle under the muzzle and awarded Wendy his most beneficent smile.

We were lounging on the wall of the terrace, the feeble rays of the autumn sun not quite warming us. "Let's take a walk to our staging area," I said. We four rose, ready for anything except hanging around the school. We shuffled past Wendy and Ruth, who sat in wicker chairs facing the Alps.

"You girls like to come along?" My voice rang alto.

"Why should we want to go where you go?" Wendy's tone could have curdled a lizard's blood.

"Forget it." How could I have clung to her that night? "Come on, Ruthie. Some exercise will do you good."

"Let's go, Wendy." Ruth skipped ahead. From the calm and assured girl who had alighted from her mother's car a few weeks earlier, Ruth had slipped into a mode of vague confusion. Even in motion her knitted brow and quizzically cocked head conveyed the presence of a pensive, uncertain soul.

"I'll go, to be with her," Wendy allowed.

I had uncovered the spot during my wanderings when I was the only student. It was a small clearing with a rudimentary fireplace made of rocks stacked loosely in a horseshoe. The surrounding woods closed in dense and dank. As I got to know each new male student, I led him to the opening, my staging area. Commandos could stash their supplies there, synchronize their watches and pore over their contour maps before mounting lethal raids into enemy territory. Parachute in, meet at the staging area, attack, then disappear into the trees. I had seen it work to perfection in many movies.

But now, for some inexplicable reason, I led the girls to my secret place in the woods, purposely destroying its status as a male sanctuary. When we arrived at the hallowed spot, there was nothing to do. Wendy sat cross-legged like an Indian, her skirt to her knees. Tony, stretched out in front of her, gazed thoughtfully up her thighs. Hermon lounged on the stone fireplace, his feet in the ashes. Dun reclined against a pine. I watched Ruth build a tiny hut of bark and twigs, "for the forest elves." Caught in the cold shadows, we said little, our eyes not meeting.

Hermon flipped a pinecone, which led to a retaliatory toss.

Soon a real pinecone fight roared. We dodged through the trees throwing and ducking. Even Wendy joined without a whine or complaint. We expanded into the forest, our shouts and laughter spreading farther and farther apart.

Alone for a moment, Wendy spun around, her face tinged with the mild panic of the disoriented. I stepped from behind a tree and hurled a cone at her as hard as I could. It thudded off her shoulder and her eyes rimmed with tears of hurt surprise. My hand tightened on another cone as my arm rose.

"What's the matter with you? You don't have to throw so hard."

At that moment I desired nothing more than to hurl the cone with all my strength. Instead, I grabbed her hand and pulled her deeper into the woods. She stumbled, almost falling several times.

"Are you nuts or something?" I dragged her until she finally sprawled on the ground, her hand jerking away. "Leave me alone. I haven't done anything to you."

I was on my knees as the voices of the others sounded far away in the clearing. I lay down beside her.

"Let's rest for a minute."

"Why are you so rough?"

"It's a war game." I wiggled closer.

"Are you a sex maniac?"

"No more than any other guy. I love—" I caught myself. Use that word only if you mean it. "—to hold you."

"But why?"

"If you'd stop talking, you'd know why." I nuzzled at her, searching for her lips. But she twisted her head to one side.

"I don't like this game."

"You liked it the other night."

"I did not!" She slapped at my arms. "You scared me to death. I was paralyzed with fear."

"Then why did you call me darling?"

"I never called you darling." She hit harder.

"I'll bet I can kiss you like you've never been kissed before."

"A real bet for money?"

"If you want."

"You'll bet me money to kiss me. You *are* a sex maniac."

"It's a game we play with the girls in Chicago."

It had been a ruse initiated by some brazen guy like Otto Minkus when Spin the Bottle became kid stuff. Like many jokes, this one had its roots in need. It proved a way to lead males and females along the same path with nickels, dimes and sometimes even quarters supplying incentive. But when it got to the point that a guy couldn't kiss a girl goodnight after a date unless he bet her first, the game was canceled by male common decree.

"That's Chicago. I'm from New York."

"Is it a bet?"

"What do you think I am?"

"It's a joke, not an insult." I loathed the whiny quality of my repentance. "Some ladies prefer the game," I tried. But I still sounded like a kid begging for a second dessert.

She heard something in my voice, however, that caused her to soften. "You are a silly face," she concluded. "Such big talk. But you're really a sweet little boy who's trying to act tough. Is that what they teach you in Chicago?"

"Please." I rolled away from her. Not motherly understanding.

"Hey," she grasped my arm. "I changed my mind. I'll take that bet." She closed her eyes and thrust her face forward, her lips pursed and sealed.

Unsure whether I should commit myself to her, I held back for a moment, but the urge dominated. I kissed her as I had that night in the hallway. It took no effort to part her lips and work my tongue against hers. She arched her back and slid her thigh exactly where it felt best.

The mountain air, the scent of the pine needles and my sheer empty loneliness acted in concert. I lost a lot of myself to her in that single embrace.

"You're so strong. You're squeezing me." Then she added, "Darling."

God, we had done it again. I was damp, and she had called me darling. Is this why I had crossed an ocean and a continent and scaled mountains, for a kiss and an intimate embrace from her? No. Never. A rare European woman of colorful language and plumage, yes. But not Wendy, not Miss Snippy from Long Island. I must have lost my mind.

I surveyed the path of escape, the trail to the staging area. In the shadows of the evergreens loomed a familiar form. The shoulders hunched, the head dangled forward, the clothes baggy, the hands driven deep into the pockets. Josh. Or was it Tony playing Josh? Had he seen us? The figure made no sign of recognition. If it were Josh he could torment me over this, maybe even expel me. Thrown out for lying beside a girl from Long Island. Not exactly what this trip was supposed to be about. I bolted upright and assumed preoccupation with a handful of pine needles. I checked for the figure but it was gone.

Wendy smoothed her skirt with her palms. "How am I going to explain this mess? Honestly, I don't know why I listen to you. I was sitting in the sun, minding my own business—"

"Hush." I placed a finger across her lips.

"You enjoy ordering me around after you roll on top of me. Just my luck to have a sex maniac in the school."

"I'm the best thing that ever happened to you."

"Ha!"

"Come on. Let's find the others."

"Ow! You're pulling my arm. Don't get bossy with me, mister."

Her familiar strident tone drove me toward the clearing as I tried to distance myself from her. But when she caught up and slipped her hand into mine, a rush of blood flushed my face. When she squeezed, I squeezed back.

Hermon, Ruth, Dun and Tony were chasing one another around the clearing. I stood beside Wendy, watching their fluent circle. A bond I had shared only with my male friends lay broken. I was with her, apart from them. Before I could restore myself in the group, the supper bell sounded in the distance. We set off through the woods.

Chapter Nine

Tony pleaded to walk with us, swearing he would keep pace. He wore his brown suede, leather-soled shoes, soiled suit and ugly tie. Not the outfit for a hike, but he managed. A bottle of local wine circulated as we sat by one of the town's gushing fountains.

I engaged Dun in one of our painful, halting French dialogues. Tony gazed at his shoes, his fingers tracing patterns in the suede. A couple of Americans passed by, guys on the GI Bill at the university. Escorting lively girls, they exuded the cockiness of victory, the casual swagger envied by every guy in the world.

Heading back, we rested at the halfway rock, the wine still buzzing.

"How about Josh not passing you the milk the other day, Tough Tony? He really is an infant."

"Rather." Tony seemed to have forgotten the incident.

"Yesterday," Dun offered, "he jumped out of the doorway at you, then acted as if it were pure chance."

"I suspect he did," Tony smiled, pleased to provide his friends amusement. "He must have told the maids not to do my laundry. When I approach them with it, they run and hide."

"He can't pull that stuff with one of us," I assured my friend. "Your mother pays his salary."

"She does?"

"Your tuition. He can't push you around. You're his employer."

"I am?"

"Think about it." The concept seemed to overwhelm the older boy as it ran smack against his English acceptance of authority. "He can't act that way with you. We'll have to teach him a lesson."

"First let's have supper," Dun said as he set off at double speed.

Meals always started on time, but tonight the large table was bare. The damp swipe marks indicated that it had recently been cleaned. Hermon and the girls were running and shouting in the second-floor hallway, and a symphony was playing on the radio in the library. As we milled in the dining hall, Josh emerged from the library, puffing on his briar pipe.

"Finally made it back, did you?"

"In plenty of time for supper," I said.

"We've eaten already, haven't we, boy?" The elderly setter raised its muzzle and licked the air. Josh ambled into the kitchen and returned with a circular wooden platter with crackers and sections of Gerber cheese. We assumed this would be our meal. Josh peeled the foil from a wedge, eyed us, put the cheese on a cracker and popped it into his mouth.

"Hungry, Pancho?" New concern for the dog glistened in Josh's eyes. "Of course you are. Poor thing can't talk. Just as well at times." He stripped the foil from another cheese wedge with infinite, tantalizing care, then allowed it to flutter from his fingers. He offered the triangular morsel to us. We strained but didn't reach, our pride still intact. The setter circled lazily under the cheese, then snapped it up when Josh let it drop.

"I thought your walking was going better," Josh said. "Yet you were late. Slowed by an extra person, I'd wager."

"We made it in our usual time," I said.

"More Gerber, Pancho?" Josh cut a peeled wedge in half

and dropped it on the dog's muzzle. Pancho chewed it slowly; he was full. He plodded across the worn tile floor to a far corner, where he turned in smaller and smaller circles until he dropped into a ball to sleep. "I shall read, then hit the hay, as they say in Chicago." He made the name of the city a sneer. "I shouldn't be surprised if I dreamed of a quiz for the morning."

As we undressed in the dorm, Hermon told us Josh had ordered supper early. He claimed that the maids wanted the evening off. Tony transformed himself into Josh, stood on his bed and cackled, "We've eaten already, haven't we, Pancho?" He patted an imaginary dog at his feet. "We're all full up, aren't we, boy?" He unwrapped a wedge of make-believe cheese and offered it toward his imaginary pet. "More Gerber, Pancho? More and more and more till you puke, Pancho?" He then burst into his maniacal cackle and shook his fists at the heavens.

In the dark, I summed up the problem. "He's trying to turn us against Tony, obviously. We have to retaliate. What can we do?"

"Pie his bed," Hermon suggested.

"That's kid stuff. This has to be *big*."

Hermon was all for buckets of water over doors and tacks in Josh's easy chair. But I searched for something masterful, European. Dun breathed easily, sounding very much asleep. Tony's bed was strangely quiet. In a moment, Hermon dropped off in mid-sentence.

"You got any good ideas, Tough Tony?" No answer. I slid from my bed to creep across the cold floor. Tony's bed was empty.

Ready to venture into the hallway, I heard familiar footfalls. I dove under the covers by the time Josh poked his head in the door. A flashlight beam probed each pillow. Josh grunted and closed the door behind him. I jumped up, hoping I could get to

Tony before Josh found him. But when I eased open the door, I saw the boy-headmaster at the closet door, listening. From inside came rhythmic slapping, a groan of release followed by Tony's pleading call, "Wendy!"

Back in bed, I pulled the pillow tight over my head. The door burst open as Josh violently pushed Tony in. The boy hurtled forward, stumbling over Hermon's boots.

"Vile, filthy animal!" Josh spat.

The springs of Tony's bed squealed as he flopped down. The room fell deadly still. Then from Tony's corner came a sniffle and a sob. I half-rose to comfort him, assure him we would triumph over Josh. But in my head I could still hear his cry from the closet for the girl. The girl I couldn't keep from holding when I had the chance. I clung to my cot.

***

Wendy examined her toast as though she had just extracted it from the garbage. She sipped her coffee, made a face of disgust and stared at the brew.

"It's lukewarm," she said in English.

Still half-asleep, I stared at her across the breakfast table. She wore her usual pale-blue quilted bathrobe. A small white barrette held her well-brushed hair in place. Round and contented, pink and pampered, she resembled one of the self-satisfied kids I argued with constantly at Hillard. They were safe, isolationist conservatives whose needs were more than satisfied, yet they demanded more and more. Wendy exhaled loudly to call attention to the fact that she was displeased. Incredibly, Josh responded with a solicitous question in French. She begrudged a tentative smile but wouldn't surrender her petulance.

"Which verbs were we supposed to learn for today?" she asked me.

"Aller, venir, savoir."
"What?"
"Aller ... "
"I know those three. I think he said three others. Tony, do you know?"
"No." Tony stared at Wendy in a daze.
"Please, Tony. Tell me."
That voice, pleading and grating. No sane male could desire this *creature*. A spoiled brat, angry if her food isn't exactly to her specifications. She makes people repeat questions she claims not to have understood, then interrupts the repetitions with her answers. Now she must think of herself as the pinup girl of all Switzerland, the female object of all male attention. The girl Tony cried for. The one I dragged to my secret spot in the woods to embrace. She speaks English at the table and still Josh treats her like a princess. Here at 7 a.m. in the Swiss mountains it all seemed a huge joke. All life was a joke if only I could deliver the punch line.

"Pourquoi souris-tu?" Her flush extended down her neck as she felt I gained my smile at her expense.

"J'ai faim."

Dun snickered. Another part of the joke: a table full of foreigners trying to teach one another a language none of them except Dun could speak.

Our life preserver in the storm-tossed sea of French was *"De temps en temps."* These all-purpose words proved their reliability time and again at the table and in French class with the crazy Monsieur Gillet. Especially with questions such as, "Do you like winter?" *De temps en temps.* "Do you like to take walks?" *De temps en temps.* Soon it elicited so many guffaws it was banned. Even the sound of *de* at the start of an answer pushed the authorities to battle-stations alert, ready to impose the harshest punishment on the wretch who had uttered the phrase.

A similar ban fell on *"Mon Dieu, il pleut."* First sung out by Hermon when a thunderstorm struck one afternoon during French, it captured the imagination of the entire student body. Not a clap of thunder could sound nor a drop of moisture fall nor a cloud pass in front of the sun without someone announcing, *"Mon Dieu, il pleut."* Gillet, who laughed at Hermon's initial outburst and sometimes smiled during the next hundred repetitions, finally ruled its use punishable by extra conjugations of irregular verbs.

Only Dun and I, however, shared the key phrase. Early on, a local guy greeted me with a word I didn't hear clearly, either *salut* or *salaud*. After Dun became my friend he explained, "If he said *salut*, it means, 'Hi.' But if he said s*alaud*, then you must fight him. He called you a dirty dog." Our greeting to one another from then on: *"Salut, salaud."*

But French proved an arduous trial for me, a grueling test of mind and spirit. For every moment of triumph when I actually grasped a spoken sentence, scores of defeats humbled me like perfect fastballs flying past my poised bat. I studied vocabulary, idioms and conjugations until they echoed meaninglessly in the crowded lockers of my brain. *"Le matin. L'après-midi. Le vent. La semaine prochaine. À la campagne."* The gender of nouns, the intricacies of possessive pronouns. On and on, prompting fits of frustration. I vowed to return home speaking like a Frenchman. My parents would listen in awe, the faculty at Hillard would be gratified, and my friends would burn with jealousy and pride. Mission accomplished; thumbs up, modest smile. I tried so hard I stammered and flailed over the simplest sentences.

At night the entire jumble reverberated in my head. The bleat of adenoidal sounds and the dancing images of strange accent marks. The classroom voice of Gillet in contention with the taunting tones of Josh at the table. The insistent Anglo-

Saxon shadings of the boy-headmaster and his mother nagged my ear, deliberately foreign in cadence. *"Duh lay, see voo play ... See voo zavay fee-nee, voo pooh-vey part-here."* It always came back to Josh and his arrogant English accent. Lost was the pure French of Neuchâtel promised in the literature. I tried to wipe my mind clear and listen for the true French voices—Gillet, Dun, the postmistress and her husband, the merchants in town. But Josh and Lily yapped as disconcerting background noise, a struggle invariably won by sleep.

The wind on the terrace carried a heavy chill. The Alps disappeared behind leaden clouds. I smelled snow in the air. I inhaled deeply and cursed myself again. I hadn't been sent to Switzerland to challenge Josh, cling to a Long Island girl and care for a guy who carried on a fantasy love life in a closet. I must learn French and how to ski well.

Gillet, standing a few feet away, obviously had lost a bout with the wine bottle the night before. His glasses tilted on his tubular nose, and his hair seemed to have been braided to a point on the top of his head. Gillet spent little time in his room, his whereabouts a mystery. With his protean appearance he could have filled several slots at the strange school. Some days he resembled a student. At other times he looked like Josh's idiot half-brother, the one who might sleep in the attic and eat Cream of Wheat with his fingers.

But his furtive lifestyle betrayed his true identity. He had to be a spy from another planet. One afternoon we boys, with Ruthie, scripted him huddled over his intergalactic radio transmitter in a hut atop a nearby mountain, calling in his reports of life on earth to his overlords on planet Zyron. We concluded that the static and interference that often swept over the school radio resulted from his transmissions.

"Gillet is broadcasting," I informed them whenever any

odd sound crackled from the radio. We would titter and nudge one another. A sure-fire means of cracking up someone, usually Tony, entailed generating a static sound in the back of the throat like a radio signal to Zyron. Ruthie, the ace mimic, developed into our champion static creator. Her creations never failed to plunge Tony into a fit of chortles and get him expelled from the classroom or table.

"Soon we ski." Gillet spoke slowly in French. "Take your holidays in St. Moritz. After the New Year, the Olympics are there."

The concept staggered me. The Winter Olympics of 1948, the first since the war ended. I crossed to the upwind side of the teacher to escape his fetid odor. Speaking French at the Winter Olympics in the Alps. That's what it's all about.

In English Literature Josh read all the parts in *King Lear* so that his students "could enjoy the richness and depth of the language." My thoughts were never so completely not with Josh. The boy-teacher stopped in mid-sentence and ordered me to pay attention.

"I was dreaming of skiing in the Winter Olympics."

To the rustle from the class Josh reacted with mild sarcasm. "The *American* has the requisite dreams of glory."

I made an exaggerated shrug that said "What can you do?"

This spontaneous gesture offered in fun touched off a blinding rage in Josh. "You ridicule me, sir! Kindly remember where you are and how you got here. You are our guest, and I for one will not tolerate this *American* casual behavior in a class dedicated to the classics. You are setting an appalling example that only a lout," he nodded toward Tony, "could admire. You will not be here for your precious skiing if you do not pay attention to the greatest writer in the history of recorded language." Josh made it sound as if that writer were he. This cloudburst of outrage caught me off guard. I backed off and Josh, puffed up with self-grandeur, resumed his recitation.

"The Jew-boy is ragging you now." Tony said as we lolled on our cots after lunch. "Ruddy slim chance you'll take to it."

"Why did you call him a Jew-boy?"

"Because he is one."

"That's right," Hermon added. "We decided, remember?"

One afternoon in the clearing we tried to trace the origins of Josh and Lily Brackbirn. We eliminated for historical reasons Huns, Vandals, Visigoths, Franks, Tartars and Mongols. The choice narrowed to Hungarian gypsies, Shinto warlords and mongrel undetermined, the last being the safest, consensus selection.

"No one said anything about Jews when I was there."

"Maybe you weren't there," Tony said.

"Even if they are Jews, we shouldn't call Josh a Jew-boy." I pressed on, upset at the distasteful turn of the discussion, not only the epithet they used, but also the realization that they had met at my clearing without me.

"But if he's a Jew, what difference does it make what we call him?" Hermon asked in his sweet piping voice.

"Josh is a person, not a Jew. He's a miserable person. But all Jews aren't miserable. How would you like to be called Chinky Chinaman?"

"I prefer it to *Hermon*."

They all laughed. I would have too, but my liberal upbringing closed its pure, clean hands around my throat. So great was the pressure, I couldn't even choke out a smile.

"I just received a letter from my mother in Bermuda," Tony said after a moment. "I may fly there for the holidays. I may even stay. It's too bloody cold here to suit my fancy."

"How come your mother gets to take so much money out of Great Britain?" I found myself angry at Tony's comfortable state.

"Bermuda is a Crown Colony. We have investments."

I checked Dun to see if that explanation were plausible. But Dun stared at the ceiling, hands clasped behind his head.

"You chaps can visit me in my mansion," Tony offered. "Everything will be free. The servants will attend your every need."

"Will there be big linen closets in your mansion?" I asked.

"I expect so. Why?"

Dun stared me down. I backed off. "To hold your suits and hats."

"I shan't need heavy English clothing in Bermuda. I shall toss them away and live in walking shorts and silk shirts."

I closed my eyes. I ripped down the sheer slope of a treacherous alp in the downhill competition. My skis chattered on the ice as I crouched in a racing tuck. The wind tore into me and I shivered, cold to the bone. I wore Bermuda shorts and a silk shirt. The assembled throng tossed derisive shouts as I sailed by.

***

The tainted remark about the Jews refused to dislodge itself. That night in bed my thoughts drifted back to Billy Curtis and Mike Straus, two of the leaders of our gang. Billy was assertive, wise to worldly ways and unafraid to make his opinions clear. Mike favored the opposite approach. Reflective and contemplative, he chose his words with caution as befit a careful student. There had been few signs of rivalry, even though they were both acknowledged leaders.

Every Saturday morning the gang would gather at Mike's

house on the North Side. House isn't the word, it was a mansion. Limestone exterior, wrought-iron portal, marble floors in the entry hallway, which was more spacious than many apartments, and a graceful stairway that swept to the second-floor social and dining rooms. The bedrooms occupied the third floor, with the servants' quarters above them. Wall-to-wall rugs comfortable enough to sleep on spread across every square inch of flooring. The bathrooms were stocked with Turkish towels as thick as welcome mats.

Because of the war, servants were in short supply. But Mike had Doc, a middle aged African-American man, who ruled as cook, butler and chauffeur. Mostly he raised Mike and his older brother because the Strauses were seldom at home. A lawyer with clients across the country and in Latin America, Mr. Straus traveled constantly. Occasionally Mike accompanied him. He would return full of exotic adventures in Mexico City or Montevideo, places we knew only from geography class. But Mike regaled us with tales about these spots as casually as he might recall a game at Wrigley Field.

An empty mansion with a savvy butler. A Ping-Pong room downstairs. A regulation-size basketball hoop mounted above the garage door. Great gifts for school kids in the city. We played there, held bull sessions and listened with rapt attention while Doc told such tales about his exploits, particularly with women, that we believed every word. We had our first parties with girls playing Spin the Bottle and dancing to Sinatra in the dark. The Strauses' hospitality became like a God-given right. But in ninth grade, rumblings shook Eden, the instigator, Billy Curtis.

"This school is becoming a *schul*," Billy announced one afternoon as we dressed for basketball practice. Seeing that I wasn't following, he added, "If we didn't have restrictions, they'd own the place like they own everything else."

"Who?" I laced up my sneakers, not anxious for the answer.

"You know who, Douglas. Hell, maybe you don't." Billy lowered his voice and edged closer on the locker room bench. "You have any idea how many Jews are here? Sure, the obvious ones like Straus. But there's plenty of others who are passing."

An illuminating thought struck Billy. "Your own little sweetie, Joy Moody. She's a Yiddische mama hiding behind a crucifix. You didn't know, did you?"

"I never thought about it. Who cares?"

"You defend the Jews. But they stick together no matter how close you think you are to them. They back anyone in the clan before you."

"That's bullshit."

"You'll see. My family warned me, and they were right."

"Well, my family told me talk like that was pure crap. And *they* were right. I don't think your way."

Billy dismissed me with a wave. "Yeah, well think this way. Fight for the ball. Guy your height should grab more rebounds. I can't do it all."

"I don't want to pick up fouls."

"Pick 'em up. Make 'em respect you."

But during practice, I hung out in the corner of the court, popping my two-handed set shot. Billy emerged from the pile of bodies with the rebounds. The coach patted him on the back while exhorting the rest of the squad, "Do what Curtis does under the boards."

One Saturday right before school let out for the summer we were playing pickup baseball in the park near the Straus mansion. Tension hung in the air between Mike and Billy, a residue from slights and comments exchanged in recent months. Both had matured into young men, their voices changed, their attitudes as squared as their broadened shoulders. While Billy muttered at Mike as he pitched batting practice to him, Mike answered by swinging as hard as he could, aiming to drive one back at the mound. It was only a question of time before someone was hit. Billy plunked Mike in the ribs and as the batsman doubled over, Billy taunted, "Stand up and I'll do it again."

Mike dropped the bat and ran toward the mound, grimacing from the pained ribs. Billy met him halfway. They collided, throwing punches. But the fight soon dissolved into a wrestling match with both rolling in the dust.

I dove in to pry them apart. In fact, the entire skirmish couldn't have lasted more than a minute. But however brief, it was an event that changed everything, a moment when sides formed. Billy, flushed and furious, shouted at Otto Minkus and Buddy Miller and me: "Choose your side. Him or me."

When Mike Straus caught my eye, I turned my head. Mike spun toward his house before I delivered my rebuttal. "We're all in this together. What's to choose?" But Mike was out of earshot and Billy pulled on his jacket while regarding me with disgust.

At the first opportunity, I assured Mike that Billy was full of it. He would cool off and it would be like old times again. "Who cares what religion anybody is?"

"It's OK," Mike said. "You're a good man, even when you're not drunk," one of Doc's classic sayings that made us both smile.

But my lapse of not leaping to Mike's defense that Saturday morning caused my stomach to clutch in the Swiss night. I couldn't allow this idle slander about Jews to continue. It wasn't right, even when applied to Josh. We would fight him fair and square.

Chapter Ten

I knocked on the library door. When there was no answer I pushed it open to find the room empty. My stomach flipped as it usually did when Josh toyed with me. I could have walked away, taken off for town as planned. But there was an elemental pull between us; he felt the need to engage me and I was primed for engagement. I climbed the wide, curved staircase to tap on his bedroom door.

"Who is it?"

"It's me, Hank."

"It's me, Hank, is it?" No attempt to veil the mockery. "What is it?"

"You told me to meet you in the library." I calmed myself. Getting mad at the start would play right into his hands. The door jerked open, and Josh stood before me in white shirt, tie, undershorts and dark socks. In one hand he held a dress shoe. Lily sat on the edge of the bed, her shoes kicked off, one leg tucked under her. She examined her cigarette, giving it more importance than my presence.

"I'm in a tear," Josh said. "Must be in town shortly, so get on with it."

"You asked to see me."

"It's Saturday afternoon, man. Oh, well, can't quarrel with a dogged American, everything according to his schedule. All other plans tossed to the winds."

I dropped into a chair. My eyes ran along Lily's legs. I cursed myself for gazing, but she was shapely. Posed on the bed, one leg extended, her skirt taut over her hips, the hem riding slightly above the knee. She gave one of her begrudging girlish smiles, recognition that I had noticed. Her air of sophistication, her pose, the awareness of her effect created the image of a pinup girl now a woman but still possessing her youthful curves.

"About your holidays, Gillet says you're interested in St. Mortiz."

"St. Moritz?" I almost bit my tongue. Daydreaming about a mother and headmistress. Losing the edge while engaging Josh was really bush league. "Yeah, but I have to learn to ski well first."

"We plan to take the school to the Olympics next semester."

Aware of being suckered, I couldn't suppress the excitement. "Golly!"

"Golly, indeed." Josh winked at his mother to affirm their common superiority—their old trick from when the three of us were alone at the dining-room table. He drew a pair of slacks from the closet and slipped them on, tucking in his shirt and buttoning up. Then he turned to his mother and recited a passage from *King Lear* while she smoothed and adjusted his clothing. They had evolved an exchange. If Josh would be the dutiful student, she would keep him preened.

He slipped on a shoe and extended his foot toward me. "I say, would you tighten my laces like a good chap?"

"I strained my back and can't bend over," I fibbed.

Josh showed no response but swung his foot toward his mother who tied it with dispatch. They repeated the procedure with the other shoe. "I have to run. Take up your problem with Mrs. Brackbirn." He adjusted his tie and swung his coat around his shoulders like a cape.

"*I* have nothing to take up with anyone."

"Really? Then I shall be off. Grabbing the funi?"

"I'll walk."

He spun toward the door, his coat swirling. Then, snapping his fingers, he swept back to his mother and kissed her on the lips. Again his pretense of nonchalance added to the performance. He had the routine down perfectly, acting preoccupied while he built toward the point of it all, to kiss his mother on the lips.

"Having a farewell drink for Tony?" Josh hovered at the door, slapping his pockets to make sure he had everything.

"Where's Tony going?" In a flash it was all clear, the reason for the meeting.

"To Bermuda, actually. His mother wrote for him."

"I don't believe it."

The young headmaster's face darkened. "I don't give a damn what you believe. It's the truth."

"No, it isn't. You're throwing him out, and you need me, I mean the boys, to agree to it."

"Are you quite mad?" He huffed a false laugh. "When I wish to throw out, as you say, any student, paying or otherwise, I shall jolly well do it. Without asking for a popular mandate from the other ruddy students."

I had anticipated this administration line, and my refutation formed on my lips. But Josh bore in. "Things are happening in our institution my mother and I do not find favorable. We expect adolescent boys to be strange. Subhuman, you might say. But even the most indulgent American private school master would not be as lenient as I have been of late. You must be aware of what's going on here. You have your nose in everything."

"The four guys stick together. If one goes, we all go." I expected Josh to lash back, denigrate me and our silly clique of foreigners. Instead, he reacted with hurt, his pained expression real. For a sickening moment my insides softened as I suffered from the old problem—feeling sorry for the enemy.

"One tries to be understanding," Josh lamented. "But you're a closed society." He slumped, his expression a mask of defeat and disappointment. I recalled the adversity faced by the guy. The tough economic times that deny him students. His dream of a thriving academy crumbling. I struggled to keep from extending a hand in sympathy. "There is abuse here," Josh continued. "I mean that in every sense of the word. Or am I being too subtle for your American mind?"

I said nothing, trapped between suspicion and empathy.

"Damn you!" Josh's pose of pained oppression passed in a wave of agitation and anger. My heart rose as my indecision dissipated. We were back on the familiar emotional battlefield. "You seem to understand everything but the most obvious. Is that why they sent you over here?"

"Sit down, son." Lily's voice was cool and measured. "You have not made yourself entirely clear."

"I shan't apologize," Josh pouted. "He knows what I'm talking about. Tony has been caught in the linen closet."

I voiced the fear felt since I heard Tony call her name. "With who?"

"By himself, you clod!" he barked. But the revelation comforted me. My secret pleasure drove Josh to raise his voice even higher. "For that and other reasons, he shall join his mother in Bermuda." Lily's cough broke Josh's diatribe. "*May well* join his mother," Josh corrected.

Once more, the surge of triumph engulfed me. Single-handedly I had staved off another purge of Tough Tony. No bribes of the Olympics or future glories deflected me. I stayed riveted on the goal—victory in every struggle, major or minor, with Josh. I heard the applause of my classmates at Hillard rattle in my ears.

"That will be all," Lily chirped.

Halfway out, Josh called after me. "For your own good I shouldn't be concerned with the likes of Anthony Heath-Merriweather. Surely a boy with your advantages, even in the United States, has seen his sort come and go and when gone never missed."

"By the way." I exuded the heady confidence of a winner. "There was no need to have supper early to turn us against Tony. It won't work."

Josh huffed his big, phony laugh. "Get on. Why should we stoop to early supper? Hardly worth it for all the whining we hear about a missed meal. You'll learn to walk faster to get your supper."

I raced down the stairs two at a time, burst outside and soared down the mountain road, my fixation with power blinding me to the landscape. Josh had attempted a European power play, the kind that had splintered the Continent and ignited war after war. But I grew with every challenge. The day could be seen when the school, in effect, would be *mine*, the Brackbirns unable to make a move without my approval. The purpose of my European mission became clearer. I was the postwar American expeditionary force bringing democracy and fair play to a broken Continent. I sang with satisfaction and achievement.

Tony's glistening head of red hair hung like a weak flare among the Saturday crowd. I caught up with my buddies in front of the ski shop.

"Did Josh throw you out of school?" Hermon asked.

"He tried, but I told him I'd cut off his allowance and he backed off."

"What did he want?" Tony looked as if he knew.

"Let's *all* buy skis. No one has to go to Bermuda."

"Then I shan't be going?"

"Did your mother write for you?"

Tony assumed his withdrawn air, silence his mode of survival.

"Of course she didn't," I concluded. "We're all finishing this school year together." Then from my memory bank popped a catch phrase from Hillard: "Take it easy, greasy. It's a long slide home." American vernacular ascendant on the cobblestone lanes of Neuchâtel, Switzerland.

"Too good to say hello?" Wendy's voice crashed like a cymbal in my ear. She shouted across the skis in English while the Swiss shoppers wheeled toward the abrasive outburst. "Getting your skis for the Winter Olympics?" Why did she yell like that? "Well, same to you, Mr. Stuck Up."

She flounced toward the rear of the store, examined some woolen mittens, then sneaked a corner-of-the-eye look at us boys. Tony gaped at her, his arms stiffly at his sides as if awaiting the next whiplash. I decided to give her a break and speak to her. But she wasn't concerned with me. She and Tony stood with their eyes focused on each other.

Chapter Eleven

"To ski well, one must be in excellent physical condition," Dun announced. "We must prepare for the snow."

"Have you skied a lot?" I asked, sure that he had.

"Never, actually."

"But what you say sounds right."

Dun ended the dialogue by bolting, running up the side of the mountain and crashing through the forest like a crazed animal. Again guided by the ethic that enjoyment without first suffering is hollow, I followed Dun's lead. The harder we trained, the more fun skiing would be.

During one of our workouts we found ourselves near a vacated summerhouse not far from our clearing in the woods. Bursting with the assertion that running up and down a mountain breeds, we scouted an unlocked window, forced it open and crawled through. In layout the house resembled a scaled-down version of the school château. A small living room with a little sun porch attached; stairs leading to a low-ceilinged second story of partitioned rooms. The simple furniture was draped with sheets, and the place smelled slightly sour from lack of ventilation. Dun sat on a covered sofa, leaned back and placed his boots on the shrouded coffee table.

"So the Brackbirns were going to give Tony the heave-ho and you talked them out of it," Dun said.

"I told them if one went, all four guys would go," I said, my voice tentative. Dun seldom initiated discussions of school politics, and there lurked more than a hint of distancing in his opening statement.

"Did you?" Dun exercised the British manner of phrasing a question as a brief declaration.

"We swore we'd stick together, remember?"

"Did we, now?"

"Sure we did. You wouldn't stand by and let them heave Tough Tony." I took the smoke Dun offered from his pack of Gauloises. "We can't let them push us around, Dun. We all agreed."

Dun's grunt didn't constitute a ringing endorsement.

"You think I went too far?"

"I didn't say that."

I lit up and lay back in the covered armchair, my long legs poking under the coffee table and my head tilted awkwardly against the chair back. "Someone has to stand up to them. I know I've got a big mouth. But in this case, I'm right. When I'm right, I defend my position."

"So you do," Dun agreed.

"I debate the Brackbirns in my mind. About keeping Tony. About keeping all of us. I tell them it isn't our fault their school has only six students. They should be grateful they have us rather than pick on us. It isn't our fault that Europe is broke after a world war. The way they act will only lead to another war."

"So they're about to initiate World War Three."

"If all of us foreigners thrown together on a mountaintop can't get along, then wars will continue as long as we live."

"Well, we don't get along badly," Dun said.

"The boys get along great. But when I debate the Brackbirns I tell them that everyone has to be friends—students, administration, teachers, maids and, of course, dog."

"What do they say to that?"

"They're struck dumb. Destroyed by the weight of my arguments."

"Jolly good," Dun said, smiling. "If you continue, World War Three shall definitely be prevented."

"In my mind I always win. But in real life, it's sometimes hard to tell who wins and who loses. I mean, Josh and Lily are so ... " I strained for the word that described their odd behavior. "So ... "

"That they are," Dun concluded. "Did Lily ever speak to you?"

The question was so unexpected I couldn't be sure I had heard correctly. It wasn't in his nature to pass judgment or to gossip.

"Speak to me about what?"

"Personal matters."

"No. She's never even called me by name," I said.

"I didn't think so."

"Has she spoken to you?"

Dun gazed off toward the exposed rafters and gave a grudging snort. "You might say."

"What's she said?"

"Someday," Dun said rubbing a hand across the back of his neck.

"She said, 'Someday'?"

"Let's clean up. Always leave a place looking better than when you found it." Dun scooped up the cigarette ashes and fluffed up the dust covers while I tried desperately to get the topic back to Lily.

"Did she seek you out?" I sounded like some two-bit lawyer doing a cross-examination.

"You might say," Dun allowed. "It's happened before."

"She's sought you out before?"

My eager, childlike tone and questions echoing in the deserted house made Dun smile paternally. "She likes to speak French with me. I wondered if she spoke French with you."

"She never speaks to me in any language."

"Small matter." Dun remained noncommittal.

"If she seeks you out and speaks French, it's a large matter, I think."

"Do you?"

"Do you like her? I mean, as a woman." I pressed on, anxious to explore this subject with Dun. "She's not bad looking."

"You noticed that."

"The other day, sitting on her bed. With her legs crossed. I mean, she looked like a girl out of *Esquire*."

"Is that good?" Dun asked with a tolerant smile.

"Sure. Pinup girl."

"Lily. Pinup girl."

"Seems crazy, I know."

"Maybe not so crazy. Must be off."

For me the conversation was just beginning to get interesting. Dun had actually offered a morsel from his personal life. But he might as well have been speaking French, as he had by the lake and on the road up from town. He tantalized then withdrew, leaving me at odds. He was trying to communicate on an intimate level but couldn't. I felt I was thwarting him, responding like a child rather than a man of the world.

"Dun, I'll listen to you on any subject any time."

"I'm jolly well aware of that." He spoke in a staccato, businesslike way, which indicated an end to all intercourse.

But I persisted. "Dun. With Tony. With everything. I mean, us four guys stick together, don't we?" He tilted his head as if hearing something new. "We're united against them. They can't divide us." I was restating what I felt had long ago been established. "We won't sell out one of our own to please the Brackbirns."

I expected a quick endorsement of this basic belief. I

thought I saw Dun nod in agreement. But his words had an edge: "Watch out for yourself."

"In what way?"

"Just beware."

"Of the Brackbirns?"

"Your way isn't their way."

"What have you heard?"

"I've not heard anything."

"Are they mad at me for standing up for Tony?"

"They are not people to trifle with, is my point."

"I'm not trifling. I'm standing up for what's right."

"So you believe," Dun said.

"You don't believe I am?"

"What I believe makes small difference. Let's not see anyone get hurt."

"I don't want to hurt anyone, not even myself."

"Good lad." Dun's voice carried a clipped finality.

We closed the window, leaving the house for other ghosts to occupy.

***

The school drowsed in stillness, overtaken by the afternoon. I wandered into the boys' dormitory to attack poor Molière. Sylvana, one of the maids, knelt by my cot removing my clean laundry from the large oval wicker basket that she kicked along the floor from bed to bed.

"It's foggy today," she said.

"It's foggy today," I responded. The phrase now constituted a ritual greeting, like rhinos rubbing horns when they meet on the veldt.

She rose, unshaved legs apart, feet planted, smiling at me with brown, square teeth. Her stance and placement precluded access to my footlocker. I nodded and grinned, as do those who can't communicate, and backed toward the door. Seeing me fade away, she leapt toward the laundry on my cot and waved a pair of my jockey shorts as she delivered a series of hisses. Unsure of her meaning, I smiled more broadly until my cheeks ached, my head bobbing as if afloat. Displaying the shorts she gestured to the place where the deposit of semen had lodged to dry.

She shook a finger back and forth like a metronome as she indicated the shorts. Then pointed to herself and nodded vigorously. "OK," she said. It was all settled. She seized my hand in her powerful grip and pulled me toward the flight that led to her garret quarters.

"You don't understand," I tried, my anxious voice squealing like the screech of brakes on a quiet Sunday morning.

"OK, GI," Sylvana answered. Her hand, rough from a life of labor, tightened on mine, her determination the pride of a vanished but not forgotten Roman Empire.

The school lay in such quietude any words would be a public broadcast. I climbed the stairs behind her. Sylvana would soon discover the source of my reluctance. I could press against schoolgirls in playful kissing sessions, but the real thing remained a hope of the future. A grown woman would be disappointed. If only I could speak some Italian, just a few key words.

The two maids' cots were placed in tandem and hastily made, wide triangles of sheet poking out from the corners of the blankets. Breaking the silence came the tink of a Ping-Pong ball and a distant cry and shout. At least someone was stirring. Still time for some kind soul to set the château on fire or at least call for a fire drill. Hey, we've never had a fire drill. If the Swiss fire prevention authorities got wind of that, the school could be in serious trouble. A fire drill must be ordered tout de suite.

Sylvana pulled me down on the bed beside her and pressed her face against mine. Her grip on my shoulders commanded, yet her lips felt feminine and inviting. The strength and toughness she exuded as she toiled around the school now melted into tenderness. She pulled off my jeans then removed her cotton dress with practiced dispatch. The touch of her naked skin, surprisingly soft and sweet, sent a bolt of new excitement through me. This was the real thing with a passionate, willing female. I tried to appear suave, accustomed to these encounters. But I soon found that my best approach was to follow her lead.

My previous girlfriends had all been fully clothed beginners who reacted on repressed instinct, mimicking movie stars playing out love scenes. Sylvana, however, was experience incarnate. Nothing fazed her, not my unsure touch, not even my immature loins. She deftly guided and directed, her ministrations so skillful I actually believed I knew what I was doing. My pleasure occurred quickly without notice to anyone but myself. In my previous experiences, this was when I rested, confident that my contentment was enough for both parties. But Sylvana didn't play by those blind male rules and continued her manipulations. She adjusted and labored, shifted and rearranged until finally, her taut body quivered and she uttered a sharp, shrill animal shout, then slumped not so much in bliss as in completion of a physical task.

The entire canton of Neuchâtel must have heard her. I expected the doorway to be ringed with the curious faces of the student body and faculty. Lily would be watching, her lips forming the famous phrase of completion, *"Si vous avez fini, vous pouvez partir."* Josh would be cradling his black-box Brownie taking snapshots as he had the afternoon we unloaded firewood, his derisive smile forcing us to recede, the butt ends of the stacked logs surrounding our faces like a hostile mob. Dun,

Tony and Hermon would cry out "Hooray for the Swiss English *Bombing* Academy!"

Sylvana slapped my butt not once but twice. She spoke into my ear in what should have been Italian but sounded like German. In frenzied speculation I wondered whether I had been lost in lust with a German national, maybe a Nazi war criminal passing as an Italian maid in Switzerland to avoid her judgment at Nuremberg.

My mind was addled with the uncertainty of what we had accomplished together. But with a few moments of rest, sanity exerted its comforting embrace. I heard Italian phrases in her familiar throaty tones. A sense of raw achievement rolled over me. Something had happened, something never before known to me, although I was unclear what. This much emerged from the confusion: I was the American, the future of the world, who, against the overwhelming odds stacked against him by nature, had tamed a tempestuous Italian beauty. Well, not a beauty, but tempestuous.

In the tumult, the pillow had fallen to the floor exposing a rosary, which dug into the back of my neck. As I extracted it, Sylvana issued a brief bark, snatched it, put it to her lips and rattled off a few clipped sentences in Italian. She slipped on her flimsy dress as deftly as she had taken it off.

Before the mirror on her bureau, Sylvana fought a comb through her gnarled hair, to no avail. Certain that the student body would be waiting to greet me in the hall, I opted to throw wide the door with a flourish. I'd be expelled like a champion. But when I swept open the door, the dim hallway revealed no one. Before I stepped out, Sylvana seized me from behind, her arms like a clamp around my waist.

"I love me," she breathed in her heavy voice.

"I love me too," I answered.

THE SEA OF CLOUDS

I reached back in embrace, and my hands fell on her hard and muscled rear. A few minutes earlier it had been as buoyant as the sea.

As I approached the dining room, I reveled in the smug derision of a criminal who has gotten away with something and is now visiting his less fortunate compatriots behind bars. I wallowed in self-satisfaction. But I forgave myself considering the circumstances. I was learning that self-deception following lovemaking was a great comfort.

In the sun-porch classroom Hermon and Ruthie struggled to hit the Ping-Pong ball over the net to each other. In the library Josh slouched in the old, overstuffed chair reading, his feet propped on the radio cabinet. He gripped his pipe as he scanned the pages, his lips moving in rehearsal of his lines for English Literature class. Wendy and Tony were playing Parcheesi at the dining-room table. As she rolled the dice, Wendy chatted, while Tony sat with the calm of Buddha. As I approached, Wendy gave no sign of recognition. When she reached for the dice, she went out of her way to touch Tony's hand, and he flushed scarlet.

"Why, Tough Tony," she teased. "Look at you blush. Isn't that *sweet?*" She grasped one of his fingers and shook it playfully.

I stepped forward to interrupt their game and reestablish myself with Wendy. This flirting with Tony was getting serious. I couldn't stand by passively. That was the role of people like Tony.

But returning as I was from my liaison with a European siren undercut my sense of righteousness. I placed a hand on Tony's shoulder and tried to catch Wendy's eye as if to say, This is my buddy you're fooling with. But this attempt at command couldn't deaden the jealousy that pierced me. Catching her with Tony never failed to elicit a physical reaction—hot flash, cold guts. Fear of losing her. Uncertain if she were mine to lose. I heard Lily's laugh as it floated from a distant portion of the château, followed by her signature cough. It occurred to me that Dun wasn't with us.

Chapter Twelve

It lay before me on my cot, a gift from another time, another place, another world. The handwriting on the brown paper was familiar, yet printed instead of the usual script. The stamps told of their origin in recognizable form, no graven images of strangers in ancient dress, no denominations in unaccustomed currencies highlighted with odd signs and abbreviations. This was a parcel from the homeland, the return address so much a part of my life that I longed to be there. These packages from home, arriving regularly as they did, always fed the need to escape I was trying to smother every day in the odd little school.

I untied the cord and unwrapped the bundle. My mother's letter, several cursive pages, lay on top. Nestled in the protective wadding of the *Chicago Sun* were a tin of tollhouse cookies and a couple of bags of quality coffee, good coffee being hard to find in Europe. I always handed the coffee over to Lily, since I lacked a place to brew it. Lily, in turn, locked the bags in a kitchen cupboard reserved for use by the faculty. The students settled for its aroma floating out of the library after dinner where Josh, Lily and, *de temps en temps*, Monsieur Gillet sipped in splendid solitude.

Usually my mother included a surprise bonus. This time she had tossed in two gaudy, hand-painted silk ties and, beneath them, bundled in newspaper, a regulation-size, hard-as-a-rock Chicago softball, which when playing back home we used without benefit of glove. To me, my mother was in that dormitory room, bucking me up with playful tokens that connected us. I knotted one of the ties around the collar of my plaid flannel shirt, ready for adoration by the others. Tony leaned toward the sliver of silk and examined the painting of the V-shaped flight of ducks over a frosty lake before a setting sun. He reached toward the tie, fingers trembling with excitement.

"Are those ties dear?" he managed to inquire.

"Sure," I kidded. I almost added "My mother sent them as a gag," but this was no joke gift to Tough Tony.

"Surely gangsters wear ties like these."

"Course they do." I busied myself smoothing out the pages of the *Sun* to peruse them for local news.

"But I wager Jews wear them too."

"Why are you so worried about what Jews wear?"

"I won't wear what they wear."

Before I could reaffirm my stand against such blatant anti-Semitism, our balcony window flew open, accompanied by a sharp blast of wind. Josh entered screaming. "Who has it? Who stole the bloody book for nighttime activities? I demand a full confession. Now!"

We froze in place, not sure what Josh was ranting about. After a few seconds I stepped forward, my hands straightening the hand-painted tie. "What seems to be the trouble?"

Josh raised an arm. I winced, certain I was about to catch one across the bridge of the nose. But the hand held. "The trouble, as you so commonly put it, is that someone has made off with my copy of *Moll Flanders*. I daresay you have never heard of it."

Since I wasn't aware of the work, I struck the stance of the silent sage.

"One of you *gentlemen* stole it for your nighttime exercises. I shan't tolerate such behavior over an English masterpiece. I shall start a search right here and now." He crossed to Tony's footlocker and began hurling out the foul socks and underwear. "God, what a stench. Abominable!"

For once Josh was right. The smell made us wince. But the boy-headmaster knew where to burrow. Barely had he penetrated the middle kingdom of the trunk when he reaped his reward.

"There you are!" He held the book aloft as a dentist with a troublesome tooth. "My instinct is infallible, as usual. This one had secreted it among his filthy undies." He whirled toward Tony, shaking the book in his face. "Tell your friends why you stole it."

"I've never seen it before, actually." Tony wore his nothing-bothers-me face, but his hands nervously clutched the seams of his baggy bell-bottoms.

"Liar! You stole it for your evening work." Tucking the book under his arm, Josh wheeled toward the window, considered the frosty breeze, thought better of it and stalked out the door.

Low in the trunk, pasted against one of its sides, clung a worn photograph clipped from a magazine. I could see only the top margin and a bit of the haircut, but that was enough.

"Who's in that photograph?"

"What photograph?" Tony kicked down the lid of the trunk.

"The one under here." I lifted the lid and pulled away more clothes. The image was faded and browning with age, but the horrid face of Hitler was unmistakable. The smell and revulsion combined to make me gag.

"How could you keep a picture of *him?*"

"He did some good things."

"Like bombing London. Or did you escape to Bermuda?"

"I was in the country outside London. It wasn't pleasant."

"Then why?"

"The war wasn't the only thing. He brought order and stability."

"Oh sure! Just a few minor problems. Millions killed. Cities and civilizations leveled. Concentration camps. But you wouldn't mind them as long as there were Jews inside."

Tony rubbed a finger over a facial pimple, his eyes jerking in their sockets. "That isn't what I meant."

"What did you mean?"

"I don't know."

I threw up my hands and turned to Dun and Hermon for their approval, but they remained impassive, staring at the trunk. The stink of the dirty clothes filled the room.

***

Alone on the sloping front lawn, I tossed the ball, intrigued by its arc in the afternoon sun. The sharp sting of the hard leather recalled cold spring games where snaring the ball without a glove was a rite of passage. In a while the others shuffled out, their tea finished, the remaining hour of daylight theirs for the taking. Hermon snatched the hat from Tony's head and threw it to me. I offered the hat but when Tony reached I couldn't relinquish it. Instead, I flipped it to Dun. Around and around Tony ran like a wooden soldier on stiff legs.

"Give him back his hat," Wendy demanded from the terrace.

"Why do you care about him?"

"You're acting like children."

"We are children," I said.

"You act like a baby."

"Why are you so worried about him? Huh?" But Wendy showed me her back. I threw the hat at Tony. "Put it on and run," I snapped. "If I can catch you, the hat is mine."

Tony obeyed. He trotted to the side of the château, stopped to look back and when I ran a few feet toward him, Tony disappeared around the corner. Hermon howled at him to fly.

I hadn't intended for the chase to be serious, but I bolted after Tony, letting out a war cry, the way the Marines did before they bayoneted Japanese soldiers in the movies. I slowed to a trot, or I would have caught him immediately. Instead, I allowed Tony to build a lead, then I would turn it on and almost overtake him. I saved these bursts for the area in front of the terrace so that the student body, primarily Wendy, could not fail to appreciate my superior conditioning and running skill. After a few turns, however, I craved more action. I rushed to pull Tony down from behind. My warrior shout drew attention to the pending combat. The student body was draped on the terrace wall awaiting more exciting developments.

"Take off your coat," I barked at the huddled figure.

"Whatever for?"

"We're gonna fight."

"I shan't fight you."

"Why shan't you?"

"I simply shan't."

As angular as he was, Tony felt like lumped pudding under my weight. I checked to be sure the student throng could hear every word. "You're a coward. A yellow-bellied coward."

"I know that."

"Don't admit it," I implored.

"All right."

"Fight me, you Nazi-lover. Prove you're not a coward."

"I don't know how to fight."

"Fight!"

"No."

With Tony pinned beneath my knees, I called to Wendy who had chosen to study the horizon rather than the human spectacle. "He won't fight."

"Leave him alone, you bully." She refused to dignify me with a glance.

Bully? I'm the defender of the free world. I had not made clear to her the point of contention. I taunted my opponent: "Say you're sorry you have a picture of Hitler in your trunk."

Tony failed to respond.

"You love Hitler don't you?"

"No, not love," Tony allowed. This bothered me. The time wasn't ripe for discussing nuances of feeling.

"You admire him."

"In a way, yes."

That was good enough for me. I addressed my summation toward the terrace. "He admires Hitler." Directly to Wendy: "You heard that, didn't you?" This would end any romantic illusions she might have about the strange English boy.

"He'd say anything with a bully kneeling on him."

"He admires Hitler, and she defends him," I called to the heavens. The entire confrontation, which began in such high moral probity, now dissolved into a petty debate. The time had come to escalate to a higher plane of action.

"I'm going to hit him and you'll see him cry."

"I expect you shall," Tony agreed.

"You want to cry. You miss Hitler and cry for him to return." Tony cowered beneath me, his face a pale blob against the brown grass. "We defended you in this school. And you love Hitler."

"I didn't ask for your defense." Tony's lips trembled.

"How long are we going to have to carry you?" My voice rang ugly, but I couldn't moderate it. "You'd have been kicked out weeks ago if we hadn't made a stand for you."

"I don't care."

"You let Josh and Lily push you around."

"You're the one pushing me around now."

Real fights didn't play out this way in the movies. This was too much talk, not enough action. I had been ready to swing at that pasty face a few minutes before, but the flash point of anger had been smothered in rhetoric. Again I checked the student spectators. Wendy had vanished. Dun was pointing out sights of interest in the Swiss landscape to young Ruthie. At an upstairs window the familiar form of Josh ducked behind a curtain. I pulled Tony to his feet.

"Get up, Tough Tony. Josh has seen too much already."

Tony's feet scurried for purchase like a crab on a smooth stone. "You don't understand about him."

"Who? Hitler?"

"Yes. You weren't there, were you?"

"No. But what he did. You can't keep a picture like that."

Tony loomed taller than me, slouched in his sloppy suit. Tears blurred the pimples on his cheeks. He smiled the stupid, placid smile he assumed whenever anyone berated him; he gained perverse pleasure in being attacked. Tony gave no further excuse for the picture in his trunk, nor did he offer to remove it. He gazed at the ground, head hanging.

Tossing the softball again would set things straight, bring a bit of American reality to the distorted European scene. I cruised the lawn searching for the ball when I discovered pieces of it down near the lower spruces. Pancho lay with the remains pinned beneath his front paws. The setter had intently pulled apart the insides of the ball, and shreds of the cover were strewn across the hillside.

It snowed. Clinging wet flakes settled to form a damp crust that covered the past. My prayer had been answered. Snow would draw us from the tensions in the château to the tranquility of the hills. Snow would soften the clashes of personality and unite us under its soothing blanket. By evening there was enough to sled on if not ski. We rode an old toboggan we found in the cellar, swaying and pitching down the hill, running back up as soon as we rolled off at the bottom.

The entire student body partook, Wendy and Tony carrying on with me as though nothing untoward had happened the previous afternoon. I orchestrated a chant-call as we whooshed down the hill: "The Swiss English *Bombing* Academy. Forever! Together!"

The snow turned to rain before supper and by nightfall the only white on the lawn was the shreds of the softball cover. The snow went the way of the Four French Chaps, the Spirit of the Library and a student body with a social conscience, all promises drowned in the Sea of Clouds.

Chapter Thirteen

"Today we shall determine if one of our so-called students has learned anything lately. Here is a boy who steals a great book for his perverse pleasure and even incites a fellow student to violence." Josh gave an imperceptible nod toward me then pressed on. "But he is a student, or so he claims. So let him show us his scholarly side. Sir, please read aloud this sonnet for our edification. Then explain its meaning." Josh plunked the volume of great English literature on the table in front of Tony and pointed to a poem.

Tony grew flustered, his jaws working.

"What, no voice?" Josh adopted a false concern. "Too much nighttime activity, no doubt. Please, sir. Make a try."

Tony moved his lips, but no sound emerged. He hung his head so low that his forehead almost rested on the page.

"True to form," Josh said as he swept up the book. "Not much to show when it comes to English scholarship."

"I can do it," Tony muttered.

"Really?" Josh returned the book. "All right, then. We wait with pleasure." He stood back with smug assurance and surveyed the little class.

Tony focused on the page before him for what seemed like minutes, his lips moving in rehearsal.

"Come, sir!" Josh barked. "The class awaits."

Tony nodded, but a slight, sly smile etched his face. Suddenly he contorted and reared back in his chair. I thought him consumed by a seizure. Then Tony hurtled his body forward as he exploded with the most violent, convulsive sneeze imaginable. The noise of his expulsion burst in the small classroom causing Wendy to shriek. A full shower of spittle flew from his mouth, and the contents of his nose were spewed onto the sonnet. Tony's head hung over the book as he fumbled for his handkerchief, which he ran across his face, then the unfortunate volume of great literature.

Josh emitted a scream of protest so quickly that it seemed a continuation of the sneeze. "You filthy, scheming pig!" He grabbed the eraser from the blackboard tray and hurled it with the force of a missile. It missed Tony's head by a centimeter, crashing into the wall behind him.

Instead of rising to Tony's defense, I shrank back, a stunned witness. The Hitler photo; the late-night cry for my girl; a shameless, manufactured sneeze. Defending Tony was becoming a heavier burden.

***

I bolted upright, my bedclothes wrapped around my head and shoulders. I thought I smelled more snow in the air. Slowly I untangled myself and glanced at the balcony windows to check whether Josh was peering in. An eerie pre-dawn stillness gripped the earth as the sun decided whether to rise above the crest of the Alps and the countryside held its breath in suspense.

I made my way to the bathroom, passing Tony, his hair a greasy red nest on his pillow. As I stumbled back into the dormitory I ran smack into the muzzle of the pistol. Mesmerized, I watched Tony's knuckles grow white as his fingers clutched the Colt .22 tighter and tighter, the pistol muzzle quivering in the tense hand. I dropped down and rolled under the gun.

"Bloody bastard Jew-boy," Tony muttered.

I sat on the floor, out of the line of fire. Tony's eyes were squeezed shut, yet he spoke clearly, repeating the same phrase. Then the gun began to sweep around, covering all corners of the room. "I gotcha now, ya mug. I gotcha bloody well now, haven't I?" he muttered. After this brief display, Tony tucked the pistol under his pillow, assumed his customary fetal position, and slipped a thumb into his mouth.

From my cot I stared at the ceiling. Tony was poised on the precipice, ready to drop away from what little sanity remained in his life, aiming his pistol at Josh in his dreams. A real-life enactment was not a giant step away. A wave of compassion washed over me as I became the defender of Josh. I had spent many waking hours contending with the boy-headmaster, but I couldn't stand by while one of his students, even one browbeaten by him, leveled a firearm in anger. Especially when anti-Semitic epithets had been uttered. Stretched out in bed, I devised a plan of disarmament.

"Tony, did you really swipe that copy of *Moll Flanders*?"

We were swaddled in sweaters and coats against the cold night as we lay reading before lights-out. Tony unwound his limbs and stepped stiffly to the center of the room. "I would not take a book without permission," he began. "I am a mere mortal not fit to challenge the rules and authority of the—" here his voice gained in hysteria— "the Swiss English *Bombing* Academy!" He released his insane cackle, his fists shaking at the heavens.

"Josh planted it. A frame-up."

"Dat's right, Scarface. He's aimin' to rub me out."

"*Throw* you out," I corrected.

"Rub me out, ya mug." Tony returned to his cot, fell on it as though he had been shot, pulled his hat down over his eyes and drifted into his impersonation of a dead man. "But I'm ready for the bloke," he said, his voice wafting across the room. "I'm ready for any of 'em. I got me hardware."

"What would you trade for one of my hand-painted ties?" I asked.

"You wouldn't trade."

"I might."

"I don't have many things you would pleasure."

"Maybe you do and don't know it."

"Well said." In appreciation, Hermon drummed his feet against the wall. He had assumed his preferred position, feet up, shoes on, eyes on the ceiling, listening intently to the dormitory discourse. When he wished to register approval, disagreement, or any position in between, he played a tattoo on the wall with his heels. As a result, the wall above his bed was a mass of scuff marks, dark digs and prints as if strange animals milled and pawed the area at night as the students slept.

Tony leapt up and tore into his footlocker. His hands emerged with two small lead models of Spitfires, which he held aloft in an animated dogfight, machine-gun sounds flapping from his lips. They were exquisite planes, perfectly painted and rendered. But they reminded me of the war and the photograph in Tony's trunk.

"No deal." I steeled myself to drive a hard bargain in these international disarmament negotiations.

Tony dug deeper and emerged with an alligator-skin wallet. A series of plastic flaps unfolded, enough to hold all sorts of snapshots, schedules and important cards such as a bus pass and school ID. It even had a secret change pocket.

"It's not enough for a hand-painted tie."

"The Spitfires *and* the wallet."

A good deal. But I kept my focus on my objective. In my mind Mr. Ellis and the entire current events class at Hillard watched from ringside seats. I had to produce for them. "What do you sleep with every night?"

Tony's lips moved as he repeated the question to himself. "My pillow?"

"What's under it?"

Tony ran his hands under his covers and drew out the pistol. "This?"

"It's something to talk about, isn't it?"

"My pistol?" Tony regarded it as he might something that had recently died between his sheets.

"With all the ammunition for it."

"But you don't fancy guns," Hermon said.

"Is it a deal, Tony?"

Tony wrinkled up in the agony of indecision. I withdrew a hand-painted tie from my footlocker. The silk shone under the single overhead bulb. The ducks winged into the elegant sunset.

"I can't." Tony groaned in physical torment.

"It's from Chicago. Nothing vaguely resembling it in all of Europe."

"I am jolly well aware of that. But—"

I produced the other hand-painted tie. A blatant acid green in background, this one portrayed a statuesque stag displaying an impressive rack of antlers at the edge of a sylvan glade. Arrayed behind him stood several does and fawns, their enlarged dark eyes glimmering with awe and adoration as they gazed at him. "Both hand-painted ties."

Tony wailed as though stabbed and fell back against the wall. Hermon drummed his heels in recognition of the magnitude of the transaction.

"You'll be the sharpest chap in Europe," I assured him. "Two hand-painted ties while no one else on the entire Continent has *any*. Wear one around your neck, the other as a sash. The European girls will be crawling all over you. They'll think you're Alan Ladd, George Raft and Edward G. Robinson rolled into one."

"It's impossible." Tony hung near tears of torment. He yearned for those ties with every ounce of desire at his command.

"Look," I began. Now came the time to be reasonable, claim what I could and set the stage for the next round of negotiations. "One of the ties—the tie of your choice—for *all* the ammunition."

"What good is ammunition without the pistol?" asked Hermon, his irritation reflecting his role as scrupulous observer who insists that everything make sense.

"Is it a deal?" My mind raced, wondering if I had left myself open for deception and regret. Tony's obvious sense of relief did little to reassure me.

"OK, ya mug. The tie with the deer for my box of ammo."

"*All* the ammo," I repeated.

"Agreed."

Tony's joyous lilt deepened my conviction that I had been outsmarted. As Tony unearthed his ammunition, I hovered, tie in hand.

"No secret stash of ammo. I get every single bullet."

"Agreed," Tony said again without contemplation.

I checked the clip of the pistol. Empty.

"Here's dee ammo, Scarface." Tony flipped the box of .22 cartridges toward me and grabbed the tie. The ammo rattled to the floor as Tony wrapped his conquest around his bare throat.

I scooped up the box of cartridges; not one missing. A trace of confidence in the transaction slithered back. "You gonna sleep in the tie?"

"I believe I shall," Tony allowed.

"I'll put this other tie in my locker. When you want to trade the pistol, leave it there and take the tie."

"A fair deal. Very fair indeed." Tony's voice broke with glee. "It's wonderful," he crooned, as he became Josh in voice and stance. "To do business with people who have read literature from the greatest civilization the world has *never* produced. Even you bunch of scurvy *foreigners!*" His wild laughter contained more than a dash of contentment.

I lay in the dark, my eyes wide open. I had surrendered one of my main bargaining chips in exchange for a single box of ammunition and Tony's unsubstantiated promise that he held no more. Why was he so happy with the swap if there were no more ammo? I had placed my trust in him despite his record of unstable behavior. Had I been outmaneuvered in a European power play? Sleep did not come easily.

Chapter Fourteen

Dun and I could afford only the least expensive skis, but this only heightened our commitment to maintaining them. Every bit of information written or spoken by anyone who had ever clamped on skis in Switzerland sent us scurrying down to the basement to check a lacquer label or a wax consistency. The ski bindings were little more than crude cables that clipped onto modified hiking boots. Remaining steady while under way rivaled walking a tightrope down a steep incline.

Gillet, who, like most Swiss, skied as effortlessly as a flatlander walks, instructed us in the basics. But being a secretive fellow, (he had to hide his role as agent for the great potentate of the planet Zyron, after all) he believed in doing, not talking. One learned to ski by skiing. He led Dun and me on outings, across meadows, through gates, slaloming among small pines and large rocks. One afternoon he plunged us down a forest path, our skis guiding the way. The heavy branches slugged us, the snow treacherous as it thinned on the rock outcroppings then thickened again in the hollows. We followed the mad Swiss professor, our wind-whipped tears streaming, our abandon to the sport everything a boy could ask.

Gillet released a long whoop of pure joy that rang through the trees with a pagan lust prompting us to echo it over and over. Our skis clattered beneath us. Sure destruction waited to smear us against the rocks and evergreens of the Swiss mountainside. We were skiing. In a flattened field we negotiated a lurching, jerking snowplow finale. Our cheeks burned, tears stood in our eyes, and our cries still rang in our ears.

We hiked up the mountain, our skis on our shoulders. This was the way veteran European skiers did it, I figured—ski down, walk up. The hell with lifts and tows. We arrived at the school in time to watch the others on the baby slope. We thrust our skis in a fresh snow bank and leaned on our poles like Alpine guides observing a playful form of lower mammalian life.

Hermon and Ruthie slid down the hill with modulated control. Wendy, following them, negotiated the upper part. But she picked up too much speed on the steep middle area and hit a rut. She churned like an eggbeater into a drift, as Dun, the professor and I watched agape. Superior observers, we had lost our sense of reality. Only Josh responded to her cries of distress. From his post on the terrace, he rushed down the hill, his open duffel coat flapping, his professorial shoes plunging into the wet snow, his trouser cuffs filling. He scooped up Wendy, struggling before clearing her weight from the ground, and carried her across the snow fields to the school, bending his head close in a comforting gesture, his face touching hers.

My insides sagged under the weight of what I had seen. Josh had responded like a hero to an emergency while I, the American hope of the future, looked on. Heaven had sent me my moment and I had faltered. That was bad enough. But Josh had responded without question or deliberation. Josh, the show-off boy-professor who mocked and belittled us in class had risen up to belittle me on the field of action. He seemed to have made his way into the middle of my life, poking, probing, ridiculing, and setting the tone for good and bad. I couldn't shake him, this guy I had known for only a few months. I was seized by the clammy grip of jealousy and anger, jealous of Josh's response, angry at my passivity in a moment of crisis.

Wendy lay swaddled in her quilted robe, her right leg projecting from the covers. An elastic bandage embraced her knee.

"How's it going?"

"It hurts."

"Boy, you really took a fall."

"It was my first time on skis."

"You looked like some Olympic downhill racer streaking for the Gold."

"Did I?"

"Yeah. But when you hit that rut, me and Dun figured we'd have to dig a hole and bury you on the spot."

"That was a nice thing to think."

"I never saw Josh move so fast. He went running down the hill like some two-legged Saint Bernard."

"He saved me. You boys just stood there."

"We were planning your funeral."

"So you happened to mention."

"Josh only wanted a chance to put his arms around you."

"Is that Mr. Jealous talking?"

To deflect this truth, I said, "You know you're my favorite."

"We know," she said sarcastically.

"It's true. I don't care what happened."

"What's that supposed to mean? 'I don't care what happened.' To what are you referring?"

"Nothing. Forget it." I wasn't sure why I had said it. Maybe I was recalling her flirtatious games with Tony. Or the way she had thrown her arms around Josh's neck as he rushed her to safety. Maybe I aimed to transform her into the universally desired female I would ultimately win.

"I hear Mr. Jealous talking. Who could it be?"

"I don't stoop to jealousy." My voice faltered under the weight of the lie.

"I know how your little mind turns. Are you jealous of Tony?"

"Who's Tony?"

"So it is him. You heard what he did."

"Did he do anything to you?"

"Now it's Mr. White Knight. I like that."

"What did he do?"

"Tony wrote my name in his notebook and drew a heart around it. Ruthie saw him do it."

"That's it?"

"What did you think, silly face?"

A scene of Tony and Wendy locked together in the depths of the woods had blinked in my mind. In relief, I dropped to my knees and took her hand. "You're a sweetheart." I wished my voice had more timbre.

"Hank." She twisted away. "I don't feel like it."

"I can make you feel great. I've got the secret."

"Why are you always so flippant?"

"I'm still a growing boy." My sweet tenor reinforced the truth of this remark and won a wan smile from Wendy.

"That night when you and Ruthie were listening to that baseball on the radio. I passed by and I couldn't believe my ears."

"I told you, they broadcast the Series for the GI's."

"You were *talking* with Ruthie."

"I've been known to exchange words with people."

"I mean real talk. Not like you were trying to impress people."

"What's wrong with talking to Ruthie?"

"Can't you talk to others in the same manner? Don't give me that innocent-boy-from-the-Midwest look. You know what I mean."

"I should talk to you the way I do to Ruthie."

"Bravo!" She raised her hands to applaud. "Pretend I'm Ruthie. Tell me what you told her."

She patted the bed beside her and I sat. She flopped a hand idly onto my arm, her touch sending warmth through me, and closed her eyes as though awaiting a sermon or a fairy tale.

"Once upon a time," I began, "a growing boy left Chicago for Switzerland. He went to a school started by a woman and her son. The brochure made the place sound like a regular U.N. for kids. International student body. Exciting school trips to famous European places."

Wendy laughed. "Isn't that brochure marvelous?"

"Marvelous lies."

"More like great expectations."

I went on about the *De Grasse*, wine instead of milk. The white cliffs of Dover. Then Le Havre with its half-sunken ships from the invasion. Barbed wire still on the beaches with Nazi pillboxes.

My voice took off an octave when she interlaced her fingers with mine. I told her about the boat train, the arrival in Neuchâtel, the trip up the funi with Josh, and my first view of the Alps and the Sea of Clouds.

"You're a good reporter," Wendy said.

"I hope to be a good newsman like my father."

"You will be."

"I'm gonna give it a helluva try."

She squeezed my hand. "You're funny."

"Then why don't you ever laugh?"

"It's not what you say so much. It's how you act. I could never do the things you do."

"Such as?"

"Stand up to people, even if you're wrong. What makes you that way?"

"I've never been afraid to speak up. It's not some strange disease."

She slapped my arm again. "What do you think of the school?"

"Four boys and two girls tossed on a mountain with three adults, two maids and a dog. A joke of a school."

"Not altogether," Wendy said.

"What's not a joke about it?"

"The people, don't you think?"

"Of course, I'm worth coming across the Atlantic to meet."

"Of course," she echoed with mock solemnity. "You and others."

"What others?"

"Let's save that for later," she said.

"Tell me how you got here?"

"Let's save that too. Hank, I enjoyed our chat. But you have to go now."

I rose, my hand still in hers. "I hope you feel better."

"I already do, thanks to you." As I started to leave, she said, "Aren't you forgetting something?" She raised her face. Before I could react, she reeled me in. I aimed to kiss her on the cheek, but she angled her face. Her lips parted and her tongue darted inside my mouth with a wondrous tickle.

"I wish you could stay, but it is impossible." She spoke in the stilted manner of one translating from a European language. "It is necessary for you to depart. I am disconsolate, but ... Thank you for a most enjoyable evening."

At the door I ran smack into Josh who was carrying his briar pipe and his volume of great English literature. His hair was a wild tangle and his eyes had an odd, unfocused glimmer. He appeared not to notice me. Unexpectedly, he emitted a brief cackle, sounding like a loon at a lake on a very dark night. His crazed look and undirected outburst caused Dun's warning to echo in my brain: "Expect the unexpected." Then Josh composed himself, still without any sign to me, strode into Wendy's room and closed the door. I tasted mild strawberry, the flavor of her lipstick.

To clear my head I strolled down the winding road that led past the local inn. The evergreen boughs hung heavy with snow that sparkled in the moonlight. The frozen snow on the road rasped under my ski boots. The mountain air pierced and cleansed. I ached with good health.

A bulky form appeared below the boughs. I slowed my steps. Something in the shadows spoke to me—a profile, a scent, an intimate whisper. Then she cleared her throat, and I recognized the sound of Sylvana. My heart stirred as I moved toward her. I hadn't been in close contact with her since our afternoon tryst. She had made no more overtures, treating me as if our moment together had never happened. And I had held back with her; she was too much an adult. Still, there were moments when I would have welcomed her experienced embrace. Like right now.

I halted. She wasn't alone. A man wrapped in a heavy coat and wearing what looked like one of Tony's hats gripped her shoulders from behind. My insides gave a violent turn. Not Tony as a rival again. Unaware of my approach, she wheeled to embrace her companion, their breath forming a single cloud in the night air.

I kept going, head bent toward the frozen road, but I shot a look at her partner. It wasn't Tony but one of the Italian men recently imported to work the winter season at the inn. Now she had a real lover. I crunched through the crispy snow, experiencing the loneliness of the old, yet secretly satisfied because I observed from youth.

Chapter Fifteen

After supper the night before our pre-Christmas exams, I bounced down the stairs finishing an apple. As I passed the saucer-shaped chandelier dangling over the vestibule, I flipped the core into it, without motive.

A cold gray hue from the new dawn filtered through the dorm as faint shadows lined the walls. The wind whistling outside the windows proclaimed the season. The dormitory hall door crashed open from Josh's kick. "I demand that the *child* who put this in the chandelier step forward."

I raised myself enough to see Josh pacing the room dangling the browning core from his thumb and forefinger as he might have held a dead mouse. He must have been up all night scouring the house for a transgression to torture us with. He shook Tony by the shoulders bouncing him up and down on his cot. Tony responded by groping underneath his pillow for the pistol.

"It's OK, Tony. Calm down," I soothed, stumbling across the room. I prayed that Tony hadn't withheld a bullet from our disarmament negotiations.

"You animal!" Josh screamed. "Throwing garbage in the chandelier."

"I put the apple core in there," I confessed.

"Stop! You've mothered this one enough. You can't make a progressive school liberal out of this sow's ear. He's too low in the animal order."

"That may be. But I did put the apple core in there."

Josh hurled the despised apple core against the wall over

Tony's bed as he shrieked, "Liars!" In the dawn's faint light, he hunched angry and cornered like treed prey. He stormed out, slamming the door so hard the top panel cracked.

When we filed onto the sun porch for our exams, Josh sat perfectly composed, elbows on the table. The classroom of English literature was the universe in which the boy-professor reigned. The printed legacy of dead greatness provided solace from the living torment of pubescent kids. Here great works as interpreted by his living genius codified the order and authority Josh craved. The smoke from his briar pipe curled in the sun streams as his tiny band of scholars poured all their knowledge of *Sir Gawain* and *King Lear* into flimsy blue exam booklets.

In the midst of the test Lily tiptoed into the room, whispered something to Tony, who followed her out. I only half-noticed, so intent was I on recalling the motivations and exploits of those grand giants of yore. Still lost in the spell of the fabricated themes and insights expected in exams, I didn't notice that Tony had failed to show for lunch. Gillet, returning after another of his prolonged unexplained absences, announced that the astronomy exam would be that afternoon. Wendy gasped in horror and the strange professor grinned malevolently, just like Josh.

In the boys' dormitory Tony's bed greeted us like a gap-toothed grin. It was stripped clean, mattress rolled, trunk gone. I went straight to my footlocker. In place of the other hand-painted tie lay the Colt .22. As I dropped to my cot, I felt a crinkled paper under the blanket. I read aloud the hastily scrawled note:

Chaps,

I have been called home early. I think they were afraid I would break all scholastic records in my examinations so they turned me loose for now. Tough Tony terrified da mugs, right, Hank?

I shall be in Bermuda for the holidays. We have a large mansion with plenty of servants and a private pool. I hope that any or all of you will visit me there. You needn't worry about money or food once you arrive, so do come along.

By the by, I'm rather pleased I put the apple core in the chandelier. Gave me a rather dramatic cause for being asked to leave. Hope to see you next term.

Cheerio,
Tony

"Who put the apple core in there?" Hermon wondered.

"I did. I swear."

"Why does he say he did?" Hermon insisted that things add up.

"Was he tossed or not?" I consulted the note again. "'Called home early.' Why make him leave in the middle of an exam?"

"So we wouldn't notice," Dun said.

"He writes he may see us next term." Hermon dug his heels into the wall in frustration. "This is a proper mess of porridge."

"We must straighten out this mess of porridge," I said mimicking the international flavor of the discourse. "Let's get to the funi. Catch him before he leaves." I jumped up, hoping a sign of action would serve a futile cause.

"No!" Dun snapped. "It's done. Leave it alone."

"We swore to defend him," I tried.

"The astronomy exam is coming up and we know nothing of astronomy." Hermon's shoes beat a staccato rhythm on the wall.

"We owe it to Tough Tony," I insisted.

"The funi is long gone," Dun said.

"Damn! We've got to do something." I spoke out of habit as the initial protective urges I harbored toward Tony asserted themselves afresh. But no plan spilled forth. No war cry issued from our lips. The avoidance of commitment was complete. "If we want him back, they'll have to take him. Remember, we control the school." In the thundering silence that followed, I tried again. "We agree on that, don't we?" The grunts and murmurs of assent fell far short of a vote of confidence.

"Leave it!" Dun was as firm as an adult addressing misbehaving kids.

He sounded like he was backing the Brackbirns instead of his mates. We had sworn we were united against the Brackbirns, but now that unity seemed to be crumbling. But I wouldn't succumb. This is for Josh and me to settle, I thought, swaggering to myself. In spite of the reservations I held about Tony's unpalatable opinions, I couldn't let Josh believe he had bested me in the battle over Tony.

I opened my astronomy notebook to be confronted by a parade of blank pages. All that existed were a few clumsy sketches of the solar system copied from scribbles on the blackboard that Gillet had left as his spoor. Of all the scheduled classes, the wandering professor had appeared only three or four times. On those celebrated occasions, his lectures were enlivened with his crude chalk markings but delivered in the secret, incomprehensible spy language he used with his alien masters.

"Damn!" I mumbled again. The world fell so still I could hear the light whoosh of the wet snow against the windows.

***

The absence of Tony's looming, lurching figure in baggy double-breasted suits and of his impersonations of Josh, complete with the maniacal laughter, left a gaping hole in the student body. His odd departure stirred conflicting feelings in me. I would never forget the joy and relief of his arrival. He was my first buddy, my savior from imprisonment with Josh and Lily.

But he had developed into a rival and a burden with his closeness with Wendy and his unappetizing opinions and behavior.

Yet I missed being his protector. Tony provided a tangible reason to stand up to Josh. He couldn't be expunged unless the entire male student body agreed, but he had been whisked away without discussion or debate. An affront to the spirit of the library as stated by Josh the night he expelled us. Now, without Tony, I was a leader and spokesman without a cause to defend, no matter how problematic that cause. I couldn't escape the gnawing sense that I had been cheated and outmaneuvered by the Brackbirns.

Hermon and Dun packed their suitcases ready to depart for the holidays the next day. "Ring me up when you get to Paris," Dun said.

"Count on it." I had decided to dip into my meager supply of dollars to accept the invitation of a casual friend of my father's to stay in Paris. Dun's phone number was tucked away in my wallet. Yet I couldn't shake the notion that the trip wouldn't happen.

That night, the Brackbirns surprised us with a farewell meal of a small roast chicken, mashed potatoes and mushrooms. Several bottles of Auvernier Neuchâtel white adorned the table, and the Brackbirns liberated the American coffee my mother had sent, our first chance to taste it. The girls dressed for the feast. Wendy, still limping, looked very good. Her hair lacked the usual barrettes and ribbons, and a portion fell seductively across an eye like Veronica Lake. Hermon didn't fart or belch, and the rule of French-only at table was abandoned, more from necessity than decree as we chattered about our holiday plans.

Josh directed a taunt at me: "For a slowpoke, you've picked up something this term. It shan't be an all-bad report card you take back to the States in the spring. Getting away from *America*," again the disparaging tone, "helped you more than you might imagine."

I intended to steer the conversation to Tony and his future at the school, but Josh's interest centered on Dun and Lily, engrossed as they were in French. As usual, Dun grew serious and intense in that language—the only time he let go. Lily nodded earnestly, occasionally wetting her lips. I poured more wine.

"You can tell Dr. Brown at Hillard," Josh said, "what a bloody large amount of stuff you learned here. European institutional education. Incomparably superior to permissive progressive school claptrap."

"Except when there's a war on," I offered. But Josh was oblivious, his attention on his mother and Dun.

"Tell them what one can learn over here. They'll flock over like geese with their golden eggs. Must have those geese with their golden eggs." He smiled his most humorless smile as he confirmed his master plan. Prime the pump of his school with a scholarship student, then wait for the paying students to come pouring in.

Hermon nodded half-asleep at his place. Wendy gazed at her headmaster glassy-eyed from her half-glass of white. Ruthie slipped on and off her chair, playing like the bored little girl she was.

"Will Tony be back next semester?"

Josh acted as if he hadn't heard. Wendy edged her chair closer to us.

"I asked if Tony—"

"Don't concern yourself with that class of human garbage," Josh said. "Disrupting class with his moronic behavior. Performing his filth—"

"He's our buddy. He'll be back or you'll answer to us." I couldn't let Tony go without some defense.

THE SEA OF CLOUDS

Josh studied me as if I had washed ashore on a lonely beach. "What did they put in your milk when you were growing up?" He turned to Wendy. "Have you ever heard such guff?"

"He's defending a friend," Wendy said.

"To his credit." Josh corrected his attitude.

A bolt of warmth spread through me as I heard Wendy's support.

"Don't fret, my childish American friend," Josh said, his eyes shut tight as if looking at me would cause indigestion. "Your beloved Tony shall return as soon as he has demonstrated his maturity. A measure we could apply to all the male students here."

"He'll be back?" My voice selected this instant to crack.

Josh squinted sardonically. "I say, when will you become a man? Been having at it a bit too long now, haven't you?"

"You made Tony leave without consulting us. You didn't clear it with me. Us boys," I countered, struggling to keep my voice from breaking.

I expected a derisive dismissal from the boy-headmaster. But instead he bestowed on me his most satisfied smug smile. "But we did clear it, old fellow." He nodded toward Dun. "Ask your colleague." Josh leaned back in his chair and stretched with the air of a master who had set straight a naïve novice. "We abided by the rules, foolish as they were. It was you who wasn't consulted." A sidelong gleam of triumph flashed briefly toward me as Josh savored my shocked silence of disbelief.

Lily stood without her traditional *Si vous avez fini, vous pouvez partir.* She walked into the library. Dun rose, took an unsteady step, squared his shoulders and followed her. Her light cough heralded their exit as the door closed behind them. The candle burned low and sputtered. Josh roused himself and with his most casual English intellectual's slouch sauntered to the

147

excluding door. There he posted himself sentinel, arms folded across his chest. Inside, Lily laughed as Dun's voice sounded in his beloved French.

"Tell them about skiing every afternoon." Josh's voice labored to attain a casual air yet was oddly hollow without the reassuring presence of his mother. Hermon's slight body shuddered with an involuntary jolt as he slipped into slumber. "Tell them about walking to town. That will bring them over. Americans find pleasure in punishment."

Dun and Lily, together. Her son, the headmaster, standing guard at the door, explaining the motivation for my scholarship. Not sure which way to turn or how to react, I gathered up Hermon to carry him upstairs. Before I left, I heard Josh hiss, "Wendy, stop by my room for a moment, will you? Some last-minute bothers I should discuss with you."

I arranged Hermon on his cot, his feet up against the wall. Then I walked down the hall to the girls' room and entered without knocking. Ruthie was curled up on her bed, her hand near her mouth, close to sucking her thumb. She seemed fearful and withdrawn, not the bubbly child I had bantered with during the Series. Wendy sat at her dressing table brushing her hair.

"You're not going to see him, are you?"

"He's the headmaster. Must do what he requests."

"Don't be a dope."

Wendy's brush halted in mid-stroke and her entire body appeared to quiver. "You're drunk. I'll bet you can see 10 of me."

"My lips are numb. But I know what's right. Don't go to his room." I reached out to hold her protectively.

"A drunken bum at your age. Wine. Sex. You'll come to no good."

"I thought we were friends."

"You can't order me around."

"I'm trying to help you."

She softened but with such flourish it was clearly a performance for my sake. "Hank, you rush in without considering the other person." She took my hand and kissed a knuckle with the false transparency of a young woman acting the femme fatale. "We'll discuss this when we're more calm."

"If I get any more calm I'll fall asleep like Hermon."

Her vague smile did little to cheer me. "Take a nap. We'll chat later."

Furious at myself as I did it, I bent forward for her kiss hoping it would be one of her surprise French jobs. Instead, we bumped cheeks awkwardly. She continued brushing her hair and checking her reflection as I bestowed my sign of affection and need.

Chapter Sixteen

Back in the boys' dormitory, Hermon sprawled on his cot, seemingly dead to the world. Then I heard him sob.

"What's the matter?"

"I don't want to go to Bern."

"Where do you want to go?"

"Chicago. People are happy there."

I knelt beside him. "Things there aren't as great as they seem in my family's letters."

"Yes they are."

"In many ways Chicago is a real mess. We still have meatless Tuesdays and poultry Thursdays."

"What's bad about that?"

"The streets are dangerous. I get beat up by gangs sometimes on my way home from school."

"No. Life is pleasant there. My guardian doesn't live there."

"You have a guardian. What about your parents?"

"Oh, I have parents."

"Then why a guardian?"

"My parents sold me to him."

"Sold you?"

"He pays for my school, but I have to work for him forever."

"Like an indentured servant?"

Hermon shrugged. "All I know is forever. It's common in China. There were several of us at the mission school."

"Maybe your parents did that to get you away from the war."

"They're out of the war in Hong Kong, last I heard. So is my guardian, except when he's in Bern."

"I'm sure they were doing what was best for you." I couldn't tell whether Hermon was a lonely kid seeking sympathy or had exposed a painful personal truth. That ambiguity always influenced everything Hermon said.

"What difference does it make? I have to go to school, and I have to work for someone." The young man waved it away, but an aura of reflection clung to him. "Hank?"

"Yeah?"

"Remember when I told you chaps how I got my name? It's from the Bible. Mount Hermon. But I don't begin to understand it. How did I get my name? How am I like a mountain?"

"Hermon is a neat name. Not many kids have it, at least spelled that way. Be proud of it. Don't worry about what it means." As I reassured him, I heard the regular breathing of sleep. Again Hermon found refuge in his dreams. I examined the tiny face topped by straight black hair. A shadow caused by the single overhead bulb cast a darkened smudge over one eye socket, a memory of the black eye Hermon suffered the night we did something no man had ever done before in the history of the human race.

I stole down the long stairway, half sliding on the banister. Outside, I plunged my hands through the frozen top crust of the snow and rubbed the powdery flakes onto my face. On the terrace, I flattened myself beside the window of the library and edged around the glass. I could make out nothing in the dark interior. They must have left.

Then a match flared inside. In that split second I caught sight of Dun stretched out in the easy chair near the radio. He seemed alone. Then a dark form moved toward him, its back to the window. The match sputtered and died. His cigarette ember traced a slow pattern in the dark as it encircled her body. Her light cough sounded through the closed window. Dun had collaborated with them about Tony and now was collecting his payoff. Dun, our strong, silent leader, had joined them. I shuddered to the tips of toes.

When I heard Wendy answer my knock, my spirits lifted. She wasn't with Josh.

"Who's there?" She sounded terrified.

"Eet ees Monsieur Gillet. Deed I leaf my skis in zere? "

"You're still drunk."

"I may be drunk for the rest of my life."

"You will be, of that I'm sure."

"Open the door and breathe some sobering air on me."

"Go to bed. Drink some coffee. I don't want you throwing up on me."

"Yes you do. You're thinking, 'Please, God, let him throw up on me.'"

"Don't mention God when you're drunk."

"Are you all right?"

"Yes, I'm all right. But I'm sleepy."

"You alone?"

"No! Ruth is right here so don't get any funny ideas."

"God, not Ruthie! She'll tear my throat out."

"Be quiet out there. I don't need any trouble."

"I'm coming in. I have to talk to you."

"Just lower your voice."

Wendy sat up in her bed, a small table lamp burning, her covers pulled up to her nose. Ruthie slept curled up in her clothes, a blanket half-pulled over her. A calm domesticity imbued the room, shelter from a contradictory, snow-blown world.

"What is it?" she asked. Her note of fear clashed with my kind intentions. "You shouldn't be in here. We could get in big trouble."

"I only want to talk with you."

"About what?"

"Us. Where we should buy a house. What to name our kids. What kind of dog to have."

"I'm too tired for your silly games. I've had a very *intense* evening." She sounded like a temperamental movie star who hadn't yet mastered the true emotion behind her lines.

"Forget it then." I tried the exit ploy. At the door I waited for her command to stop, but none came. I turned to offer her one last chance. Her eyes stayed on me.

"Hank. Do you know that I'm Jewish?"

"No! Jewish! This is dreadful. Why didn't you tell me before?"

"You see. It's impossible with us."

"The way I was raised, being Jewish was considered good," I said.

"That's the way I was raised too."

"At Hillard half the school is Jewish. My sister and I only got accepted to balance things out. A kid on my block, Michael Prince, couldn't get in and he's smarter than me. He says it's because there's a quota system for Jews."

"You must know the truth about me."

"It's too much for a boy to handle."

"Don't you understand anything?"

I caught the sparkle of tears in her eyes and sat beside her on the bed. "I don't give a damn if you're Zoroastrian. What's religion got to do with anything?"

"I have to be honest with you."

"Josh got you all messed up tonight."

"He has nothing to do with this."

"He has something to do with everything here." I placed a hand on her forehead. "You may have a fever."

"I'm all right. I feel better now."

As I shifted my weight to keep from slipping off the bed, the cover of a notebook prodded me. "What's that?"

"My secret volume."

"So you're the one who took *Moll Flanders*. Let me see." Over her mild protests, I worked the spiral notebook from the covers and held it under the lamp. It contained mostly blank pages. Then I spotted immaculate handwriting, really embellished printing with curlicue letters, circles for dots, as neat as needlepoint.

"That's personal," she claimed. "Not for public consumption."

"OK." I handed her the book.

"Aren't you interested?"

"Sure."

She riffled through the pages and folded the notebook back on itself. "I'll let you read this if you promise not to laugh or make fun of it." She clutched the book to her bosom until I promised.

I angled the notebook to get the most light and read aloud:

Hidden behind a veil of flesh
Alone, unseen but felt.
Not answering the knocking
On the chambers of the heart.
Unreached by cries of time.
Waiting for the only voice,
The awakening by a stranger's soul.

I paused for a long moment, the back of my mouth dry with an odd emotion. "You didn't copy that. You wrote it."

"Don't laugh at me."

"Even I wouldn't be that dumb. It's beautiful."

"You think so?"

"I know so."

"I'm glad. I wrote it for you."

"Am I the only guy who ever read it?"

"Of course. It's for you."

"I'm honored. I really am."

We faced each other, Wendy propped up on her pillows, me teetering awkwardly on the edge of the narrow bed. The poem hung in the air between us, a dazzling bond of words and hidden feelings. Now she was more observant and sensitive than I had dreamed. This realization both attracted me and made me leery. I had witnessed this with girls at Hillard. They usually deferred to the forceful personalities of the boys. But in English class when they read their writing aloud, the girls could part the childish fog of bluster, swagger and comic-book humor to see into the mind and the heart. She had dedicated this expression of intimacy to me. But this declaration placed her at a remove. Showing my gratitude with a kiss or hug would be an indelicacy.

"I don't know what to do with you now," I confessed.

"You don't have to *do* anything with me. It was something I wrote." To my baffled expression, she added. "I didn't mean to make you sad."

"You didn't. I'm impressed and grateful."

Her hand slipped into mine and she closed her eyes. I leaned forward to kiss her, but froze at her lips.

"Please, darling," she whispered.

"Please kiss me, or please go away?"

She burst into laughter, something not easy to make her do. "Hank, I don't know about you. You're so *American*." It was a judgment Josh might have delivered. Her hearty response diminished the aura of purity her poem had created. I pressed my lips to hers. Sure enough, her tongue darted into my mouth. Then her cough of laughter broke the spell.

"What's funny?"

"I can't stop. Oh, this has been such a crazy night."

"What happened with Josh?"

"Oh, not much, really." She explored the far reaches of the ceiling with her gaze. "The world does funny things." Her laughter bubbled out again. "No. That makes no sense. Things happen, so suddenly sometimes." She gazed through me, as if I weren't there.

"Take it easy, greasy, it's a long slide home."

She regarded me as she might a stray animal. "Oh, Hank," was all she could manage. I hadn't a clue if she were laughing at the pleasure of my company, at my half-drunk forlorn self or at the world and its happenings.

***

Dun and Hermon whispered as they buckled up their luggage. I lay on my cot in my clothes, as I had spent the night. My two buddies were dressed to meet the world. Hermon wore long trousers and a suit coat a couple of sizes too large, Dun his gray tweed knickers and matching suit coat with the hint of a belt sewn into the back, wool knee-socks and polished, thick-soled shoes. If Dun had swung a knapsack full of dynamite onto his back and said he was off to blow up a Nazi rail trestle, I wouldn't have doubted him.

"Know what Josh told me last night?" I said hoarsely, still half-asleep. "Tony will be back for the next term."

"Well, that shall be something to anticipate." Dun sounded dubious, as if only he knew the true story. Hermon fought his suitcase down the stairs. As I swung off my cot, I asked, "Dun. Why were you with Lily in the library?" Josh's revelation about Dun still stung. I hoped Dun would reaffirm his solidarity with our side. But he didn't respond. With a sudden anger I spat, "She and Josh are the enemy."

"Who says they are?" His tone was brisk.

"We all agreed."

"Did we?"

"Yes. To keep Tough Tony in. To keep them off our backs."

"Your little war." Dun dismissed me with the back of his hand.

"Josh said they told you they were tossing Tony and you agreed."

Dun paused, his eyes on his suitcase.

"Is that right? You let them toss Tony without telling us? Is that what you meant when you told me to expect the unexpected?"

"It's more than that."

"Damn it, Dun, you shouldn't have played along with them."

"You're a child!" he snapped. Then he softened his tone and ran a thick hand through his slicked-back hair. "It's their school. I can't tell them what to do. I haven't done that well guiding myself."

"If we stand together—"

He leveled a finger toward me and said, "You don't know what's happening here."

"Then tell me."

"It's decent to try to make the world into a fairer place. But there's often a price to pay."

"I'm aware of that."

"As long as you are." But the way he regarded me gave every indication that he didn't believe it. "Remember, expect the unexpected." He smiled as if he were repeating a familiar joke. "Must be off." Grabbing his heavy bags he headed down the stairs, leaving me to decipher this strange exchange. Knowing that Dun always had a valid point when he spoke, I vowed to continue to expect the unexpected.

I ran to catch up with them as Dun pushed the wheelbarrow full of luggage to the funi. The morning blew cold with the promise of more snow.

"Ring me up in Paris." He gave my shoulder a reassuring pat, a gesture that dissipated for me the heavy air of our spat. I always felt uneasy being at odds with Dun. His approval counted for a lot.

"I shall," I assured Dun with a return tap on his arm. "Have a good time in Bern, Hermon."

"I shan't." He gave a tiny belch. "Ski well for the Olympics."

"I'll never make it."

"Of course you shall. Americans can do anything."

"Kiss Lily goodbye for me," Dun said with a wink, a true Continental toying with a kid.

"We'll tear Paris to shreds," I said. "Then what a spring semester we'll have. The four of us back together."

"Don't forget the Four French Chaps," Hermon piped. We chuckled and hit each other playfully. I wondered why the hell I continued to hang around the school. I should get away from the Brackbirns, hop on the funi and light out for Paris. But I was kidding myself. Wendy was still at the château. After the travelers boarded the funi I called to Dun, "*Salut, salaud.*"

"*Salut, salaud.*" Dun flashed a V-for-victory.

I stood on the hilltop as the funi slid down the mountain. I almost shouted, "Hurrah for the Swiss English *Bombing* Academy!" But I kept my mouth shut. As I walked back to the school rolling the wheelbarrow, my head throbbed.

Wendy and Ruthie were playing hangman in the dining room, bouncing up and down with excitement, trying to trick each other. Wendy acted like a little girl. Hard to believe she was the same female who wrote soulful poetry and sent her tongue on tantalizing missions into my mouth.

"Boy, I'll bet you have some headache this morning," she said, smiling.

"Actually, I've been up since dawn running barefoot in the snow."

"I'll bet." But she wasn't convinced I was lying.

I trudged up to the boys' dormitory, now empty and bedraggled without the others. I tucked the coveted Colt .22 pistol into my belt and pocketed the box of ammunition. Outside, I snapped on my skis and tracked across the side of the hill, the wind billowing open my Levi's jacket. Sliding through the woods my skis glanced off the snow-buried stone fireplace in the clearing.

I wondered if the remains of the letter survived under the white cover. The day after the last of the boys checked in, I had taken it to the fireplace, crushed it into a ball and watched it burn into a bloom of ashes. It was the note I had written informing my parents that the Brackbirns were strange, the school was a farce and I wanted out.

Kicking the skis free, I slapped them together, the loose snow falling off. I drove them upright into the snow bank near the door of the vacated summer house Dun and I had sneaked into. The window resisted in the cold but soon yielded. Illogically, it was colder inside than outside, the furniture covers like sheets of ice. I leaned back on the sofa, dropped my feet onto the low table and broke out my black French cigarettes. I drew the pistol from my belt and dug the bullets from my pocket. The cold wax of the cartridges stuck to my fingers as I loaded the magazine of the pistol.

The weapons are now in the hands of the Americans, the responsible people, I announced to myself. I would use the pistol. I had more nerve than Tough Tony.

I squashed out my cigarette on the sole of my boot and slipped the butt into my pocket, then scattered the ashes. From my perch on the sofa, I raised the pistol with great concentration, and fired off a round. The bullet pierced a window leaving a glistening spider web of cracked glass around the hole.

The Petty and Vargas girls from *Esquire* and gas-station calendars flashed through my mind. Those ideal female forms with precious parts covered yet available beneath gossamer wraps.

I kept firing at the windowpanes, pieces of glass flying. Finally, the trigger clicked, once, twice, the cartridges exhausted. I closed my eyes and pressed the warmest juncture of my anatomy. If only a Vargas girl would materialize. My tempestuous Latin lover Sylvana would fit on the chilly couch. Even Lily. No! I couldn't consider her. Yet Dun had overcome his reservations the night before. But Dun never had any reservations about Lily. He always expected the unexpected.

I craved someone who kept me on edge, made life interesting. The image of Wendy in her bed handing me her poem snared my attention. I smelled her sweetness, tasted the faint strawberry of her lipstick. The empty pistol rested on my chest, its acrid scent blending with the wet essence of my dream.

Chapter Seventeen

The dining-room table at supper, lacking three-quarters of the male student population, was subdued. Just me and the two girls, who clung together like a couple of birds on a winter wire.

"You just wander around, don't you?" Wendy tried to sound judgmental, even taunting, but her pleased smile betrayed her true feelings.

"I'm a spy."

"For who? The Communists in China?"

"For the Dairy League. You haven't drunk all your milk. That's ten lashes with a wet noodle."

Ruthie giggled. She and I shared an affection for corny routines. But Wendy denied any show of appreciation: "Such a comedian."

"I don't know whether to go to Paris right away," I speculated, for effect, "or make my way to Saint Moritz to limber up for the Olympics."

"Who's paying for that, if I may be so bold?"

"The school handles all my money needs. You see," I leaned forward to whisper, "I'm the bastard son of Josh and Lily."

Wendy flicked her spoon, which glanced off my shoulder and clattered to the tile floor. "How can you even think such things? You're still drunk, an evil drunk."

As if on cue, Josh and Lily entered the dining room, hand in hand, bringing all conversation to a roaring halt.

✳✳✳

When I awoke, the bare light bulb still glowed overhead. With footsteps sounding on the stairs, I presumed it was morning. But the windows were black. Josh barged in.

"I saw the light burning. Were you asleep?"

"No," I lied. "I was reading."

"That book on the floor?"

"I always rest the book on the floor upside-down when I read."

Josh paused for a moment to examine me then said, "You know, you're not bright enough to have such a superior attitude." He made a sucking noise between his lips and teeth and raised his left leg to adjust his undershorts. "Can't run up the light rates, can we? Beastly waste." He swung a chair under the overhead fixture, climbed up and unscrewed the bulb. He whistled as he juggled the hot bulb in the darkness. "Bloody thing's torrid. Must have been burning for weeks. Well, you'll bloody well read in Braille from now on. Or come down and read in the library like a civilized human. Molière in bed." He snorted in disgust as though that were the reason he was taking the bulb.

The little bedside lamp in Wendy's room defied the darkness. I leaned against the door jamb and basked in the warmth. Dainty curtains hung in the window. Frills framed her dresser and a couple of small, silky pillows decked her chair and bed. A quilted jewel box spilled open to display the glittery mementos of her years on earth. Inhaling the heady aroma of her female world, I was engulfed by a desire to embrace the room and those within.

"He didn't steal your bulb, anyway." Wendy's shoulders twitched in surprise at the sound of my voice. "He took my light bulb," I explained. "Mind if I sit here a minute?"

"I'm in a frightful tear," Wendy said again employing

a phrase straight from Josh. "But of course. Please sit down. Don't mind if I keep working. My ride leaves first thing in the morning."

"Who's your ride?"

"Mrs. Carlisle. Ruthie's mother. The one who brought us here."

"You're taking all that home with you?" The suitcases and trunks she arrived with had been marshaled by the door.

"It's a long holiday. I need my good clothes. My parents are having a holiday party on December 27th."

"At your house."

"Stop by if you're in town."

"In Zurich?"

"Sure." She was so casual I wasn't sure how serious she was.

Before I could react to this halfhearted but intriguing invitation, Ruthie gave a small cry as she rolled over in her sleep. Again she was dressed as she dozed, nestled between two small suitcases on her bed.

"She's like Hermon. Can sleep anywhere."

"I wish I could. Sleep is impossible for me until everything is done." Wendy was packed except for the jewel box. She kept pulling out bright pins and pearls, holding them up against her sweater, then returning them.

"I've thought a lot about your poem."

"Oh?" Her business ceased, and she braced to receive a blow.

Without realizing I could, I began to recite:
Hidden behind a veil of flesh
Alone, unseen but felt.
Not answering the knocking
On the chambers of the heart . . .

"I go blank here," I said. "I know it ends, *Awakened by a stranger's soul.*"

"You remembered. Hank, I am really impressed." She offered a hand for me to shake, which I did.

"It's not every day I get a poem written for me."

"That's right. It was for you."

Her casual manner set me on edge. She said she wrote it for me but maybe she'd dedicate it to any guy who wandered into her room. I wondered if it were that good or interesting a poem after all.

"I'm teasing," she corrected. "Of course it was for you." Her face softened, and I imagined that our intimacy would now return. It took so long to get her mind on the right track. She peeked at her wristwatch and chirped, "Look at the hour."

"You have an appointment?"

She shot a look of pure suspicion, opened her mouth to reply, then concerned herself with the contents of the jewel box instead. "I love to talk to you. But not always on demand." She was dismissing me.

I rose abruptly and headed for the door. We were forever at cross-purposes, Wendy and me. I wondered why I had wished for her as my dream companion in my secret Swiss chalet.

"Don't leave mad. Please." Her pout cast her as a child, not much different from Ruthie. "Come here," she ordered softly.

She closed the door quickly, then flipped a suitcase on its back and stood on it, beckoning as she rose taller. Her lips were so warm; her fingers floated across the back of my neck. "Don't be mad at little Wendy," she cooed. "She has to hold back or she'll do things she might be sorry about."

I huffed my worldly laugh, which came out a childish snort. Her lips and caressing fingers took their toll. I forgot why I was annoyed with her. My hands slipped to the swell of her hips.

Time to act, affirm my physical longing. But I found myself paralyzed. I froze in an unexpected mystical union with her. A serenity and comfort engulfed me that in their own way were transporting. We clung together for a long time, long enough for reality to return. She whispered into my neck. "You are so dear." She glanced at her watch. We eased apart and slid down to sit side by side on the suitcase. "Hank?"

"Yes."

"I don't—" She let it drop.

"I don't either," I replied. "Although sometimes I do."

She nudged me, appreciating the incongruity, but her elbow stung.

"It's late," she said as she rose and opened the door.

"I've got all night."

"I don't."

"Running off to see Josh?"

"You silly face. Wouldn't that be my business?" She kissed my cheek. "You get some sleep. I have tons of things to do. I may be up all night." She pushed me toward the door.

"Wendy, do you give a damn for me?"

"What a thing to ask? And with such language."

"How about a yes or no."

"After what we just did? A love scene right out of a movie? Sometimes I wonder what in the world goes on in that head of yours." Before she shoved me out, she let her lips run wild on my neck then kissed me quickly but passionately. "Does that answer your question?" she whispered.

I grabbed her, my hands at her waist jerking her hips close. My mouth pressed to cover hers. She reared back from the onrush, twisting and pushing me away with all her might.

"Stop! What's the matter with you?"

"Please, Wendy."

"Don't." She broke away. "What do you want from me?"

"I don't know," I answered.

"You can be so sweet, then you get like this."

I blurted out the truth. "I feel like rolling around naked with you."

"You are too much tonight, mister. Passing such remarks. Is that how boys talk to girls in Chicago? If so, remind me never to go there."

Alone in the boys' dorm I lay in tormented agony when the voice in the hall fluttered and screeched, resounding in the special niche in my brain reserved for Josh. Then I heard the affirming laughter of Wendy, shy in the presence of authority, bold in its collaboration.

My natural impulse told me to rise up and protect her. But the sickening reality was that she neither sought nor desired my protection. Wendy and Josh cavorted as I listened. Wendy. All the areas of appreciation, physical needs and raw desires clashed around her. I clamped the pillow over my head and worked my face into the mattress.

Chapter Eighteen

The shouts of the little girl dragged me from a deep sleep. "Mama's here! Mama's here!" I pulled on my Levi's and boots, thinking in the back of my mind that Mrs. Carlisle was the person to help shape my destiny.

She stood in the vestibule near the seldom-used main entrance of the chateau. She bore her privilege well. Yet as in many well-bred people, an air of uncertainty and disappointment haunted her eyes

"Ruth, dear. Please."

"She's glad to be getting out of here," I said.

"Remember me? I'm Ruth's mother." She extended a gloved hand. She wore a green wool coat with a fur-trim collar and a hat with a feather thrusting from it. Her regal dress and comportment made me want to kiss her outstretched fingers in homage.

"Are you headed for Zurich?" I failed to eliminate the pleading tone.

"Why, yes? Would you like a lift?"

"Well, you see. I have nowhere—" I might as well invite myself and demand Christmas presents too.

"What are you doing for the holidays?"

"I'm not sure."

"Would you consider coming home—to Zurich—with Ruth and me? We could have an old-fashioned American Christmas together."

"Do you live near Wendy?"

Her face turned a bit sour. "Not far."

"You sure it's all right?"

"The pleasure will be all ours."

Now I could see Wendy in a different setting without Josh lurking around. Then on to Paris. Still, reservations nagged. Getting myself invited compromised my sense of free will. But I can't read in my room without a light bulb, I rationalized.

I set about loading the car then ran up to the boys' dormitory to pack. My fingers hit the hidden pistol when I reached into my trunk. I couldn't take it with me. If I decided to go on to Paris by train, crossing the French border packing a pistol would be serious if I got caught. Leaving it in my footlocker where Josh might discover it was no answer.

A hurried search jogged my memory. In the back of the closet was a shelf ledge with a board wedged vertically as support. A hidden pocket I had discovered when I spent hours alone as the only student. I slid the pistol into the cache, followed by the box of ammunition. I tossed an old pair of rubber boots over the entrance to the hiding-place.

I slid the full Val-a-Pak across the floor and carried it to the car the way fighter pilots did when they got furloughs after many dangerous missions. They left their P-51 Mustangs or Lockheed P-38's, swung their Val-a-Paks into jeeps and took off for exotic locales and willing women.

As I came back inside, I saw Mrs. Carlisle and Lily emerge from the Brackbirns' rooms, their voices strained with fake friendliness.

"Are you going away for the holidays?" Mrs. Carlisle asked.

"No. We shall be here working. That's out nature," Lily answered. "We never take holidays."

"Yes, of course. So much to do at a school."

I rushed back to the car. I couldn't listen to Lily playing the martyr to impress a tuition-paying parent. The false measure of suffering in her voice set my teeth on edge. Let them stay here in their little school, alone together. After some confusion as to who would sit where, Mrs. Carlisle shepherded Wendy and Ruth into the backseat. She told me to sit up front. "You're our little man. You be the navigator," she explained. I obeyed without questioning her failed logic. I didn't know how to get to Zurich. But anything, just to be under way.

As we drove down the driveway, Josh and Lily observed from the main doorway. Despite the cold air, they remained in their dressing gowns, looking more like husband and wife than mother and son. Josh's hands twisted at the sash of his woolen robe, his body keyed to the next words from his mother. They didn't lift a hand in farewell, but watched the car for a polite couple of seconds, then stepped back inside the château. Josh closed the main door behind them.

I sank down in the passenger seat and squeezed my eyes shut as I lost myself in reveries. Hillard must have adjourned after its assembly of holiday music. Christmas carols and for balance a couple of Jewish songs, like good old *Hava Nagila* sung in Hebrew. The decorated Loop with Marshall Field and Carson, Pirie Scott gleaming with lights and packed with shoppers. Seasonal headline stage shows between movies at the *Chicago* and the *State-Lake*. My mother hiding packages in the back of her clothes closet. But I wouldn't be there to conspire with Peggy as to whether we should sneak looks at everything or save one or two surprises until Christmas morning.

The eternal waiting and anticipation of Christmas. The excitement of the planned visits to my mother's parents in Wisconsin. The hints of projected gifts from my father's mother when we visited her place on the South Side near the university.

I gained solace by working on a model kit, maybe an airplane—fighting planes were my specialty during the war—or a car or a sailing ship. I would spread the kit across my desk, school books relegated to the floor, and toil over the bits of balsam wood with my beloved X-acto knives and Testor's airplane glue. I lost myself in the intense concentration of constructing the model, consumed by the project as I watched it take form day by day. I could see it in my dream, feel the clear glue hardening on my fingertips, smell the heady scent of the colored dope, with which I painted it. On and on I dreamed, so pleased to be home for the holidays.

The car's sudden stop jolted me forward and my eyes jerked open. The rain slanted against the windshield as I heard the insistent tapping and the voice from outside: "Hi, dear. Have a nice trip?" Wendy's mother waved, her face deep in the shadow of an oversize yellow oilskin hood. "Come in," she shouted at Mrs. Carlisle. "Rest yourselves after the trip."

"We have to get on. We'll see you on the 27th, isn't that right?"

"Yes, the 27th. But you'll see me today too." She pulled open the car door and urged Mrs. Carlisle from behind the wheel. "Come in and take a break after such a drive." Mrs. Winner herded the women inside. "Only in Switzerland have I seen weather like this. Those Alps make strange things happen. We have no Alps on Long Island."

I carried Wendy's baggage into the house. Wendy and Ruthie had disappeared. Mrs. Winner ushered Mrs. Carlisle and me to chairs in the living room and produced cups of hot coffee.

"You're a fine young man," she said to me. "I see why they sent you over here to represent America. You're what America stands for. All you young people are." She raised her cup. "Here's to America. And very happy holidays."

I heard the girls upstairs, whispering and tittering like kids as they played with Wendy's dollhouse. Soggy and a bit disoriented, I was unsure why I had chosen this trip over an immediate one to Paris.

"We really must be on our way," Mrs. Carlisle insisted, then called to her daughter.

"Don't forget our party on the 27th," Mrs. Winner reminded her as the girls came downstairs.

"You'll be here for that," Wendy said to me, then whispered, "Hank, come in here for a minute." She led me toward the kitchen.

"We really should be on our way," Mrs. Carlisle called.

"Only a minute," Mrs. Winner warned her daughter.

"Isn't this awful. We can't be alone," Wendy said when we were behind the kitchen door. "I'm going crazy looking at you and not being able to touch you. Do you feel the same?" She was so affectionate our tussle of the previous night seemed forgotten.

"Sure I do." I reached for her waist, but she slapped my hands away.

"We can't start now, darling. I'm busy, busy, busy till the party. Can you wait till then?

"No."

"I can't wait either. But we must. That's the horror of it."

"Let's go somewhere and be alone so I can hold you."

"I'm saving hours for you after the party. I'll even write you another poem. You write me one, too."

"It's already in my head."

Our kiss was brief but her tongue did its work.

My spirits soared. My plan was working out after all. We would have time alone. I would be fervent but restrained, so caring and loving that Josh could never wedge himself between us. I grinned like a fool.

The streetlights squiggled off the frozen rain on the windshield as we drove through Zurich. The clang of tram bells broke the frozen crust of the night. Ruthie gazed out the rear window from her perch on the backseat like a captive carted away to face an uncertain future among strangers. She had been so exuberant at her mother's arrival yet so distant in her company, anticipation exceeding reality.

The door to the apartment was stuck. Mrs. Carlisle abandoned the key in the lock and covered her eyes with a gloved hand in utter frustration. I stepped forward and shouldered open the door to stagger into the strange living room. I sang out, *"J'entre dans la salle de classe."* Not quite accurate, but a French homage that sprang to mind.

The apartment was cold, but not only in temperature. Bereft of human touches, it resembled a hotel suite decorated out of necessity rather than concern. Jackknifed on a couch wrapped in a blanket, I closed my eyes and pictured Wendy at her best, soft and warm, scented like a wildflower. Sitting on the bed beside her, reading her poem, holding her hand. Our embraces spiced by her darting tongue. If only she would appear in her familiar blue quilted robe. Just this once, right now. But I was alone, huddled under my blanket.

Chapter Nineteen

A large holly wreath decorated the door of Wendy Winner's house, and the plinky music of plucked violins came from inside. Mrs. Carlisle hesitated at the door so I rang the bell. Mr. Winner, a short, balding, hefty man holding a glass of eggnog, greeted us: "Welcome! Happy holidays!" At last the purpose of my voyage to Zurich was being realized. In this spirit of happy relief, I grinned at Wendy's father then bubbled over at the sight of Mrs. Winner and embraced her while laughing too hard.

"Sam, this is the Hank I told you about. We don't have to worry about America with boys like him around."

Sam closed his beefy paw around my hand. "You got her fooled anyway. That's half the battle. Have some eggnog, young man. You're old enough."

"Old enough!" Mrs. Winner boomed. "He hauled in Wendy's things the other afternoon, then we had a coffee party."

She laid a friendly hand on Mrs. Carlisle's well-tailored shoulder to include her, but Mrs. Carlisle recoiled at the touch. Mrs. Winner continued, unfazed by the rebuff. "Yes, a coffee party. All we lacked were an orchestra and balloons."

"That's right." My voice broke and the adults smiled.

"You're all Wendy speaks of concerning the school," Sam Winner added. "She says it's your wit and humor that keep everyone going."

I recalled how hard I had worked to make Wendy smile,

let alone laugh. I decided to give them a sample. "Remember," I intoned, "it is better to receive than to give."

Mr. Winner furrowed his brow before a thin smile creased his round face. "That's funny," he clarified to the others. "That's very amusing."

A fire crackled in the fireplace and sprigs of mistletoe and other winter greens festooned the doorways and tables. A small tree blinked modestly in the corner, an overgrown shrub with holiday pretensions.

"Odd birds, both of them," I heard Mrs. Winner tell a cornered and uncomfortable Mrs. Carlisle, who clung to her drink as if it were a weapon. "Brilliant, brilliant people. But odd birds. Sam says the husband is off in Canada making a fortune on the market. He and Lily are separated but not divorced, and he sends them money by the trunkful." Mrs. Carlisle finished off her cup and refilled it. "Imagine," her hostess continued, "a husband who takes off but sends money back by the basket. They wrote me that they had wonderful plans for next term. A trip to Saint Morris for the Olympics. Not that schools should be wasting kids' time with winter sports."

Wendy emerged from the kitchen swathed in a tight red wool skirt and a white angora sweater. Her legs appeared longer sheathed in silk stockings, and she walked with a slight wobble in high-heeled shoes.

"You remembered to come," she said with a trace of coyness. I hoped we wouldn't have to play some complicated game before we could be close.

"I wouldn't miss seeing you dressed like this for all the snow in Switzerland," I said. For emphasis, I slipped an arm around her waist in a manner too forward for a family gathering. Wendy flushed and moved away.

Most of the guests were American and Swiss business

associates of her father's, men doing their importing and exporting of goods and currency in this commercial corner set aside as neutral and impartial by the powerful merchants of Europe. They reminded me of some of my classmates' fathers, uncles and brothers whose offices I had visited at the Merchandise Mart. They played bridge and made phone calls. When my mother asked what these men did I could only answer, "Make money."

A tiny thud and a brief, stifled cry. Across the room, Mrs. Carlisle sagged against Mrs. Winner, a spilled cup of punch at their feet. The other guests wore the mandatory expression of concern, but they pulled back to avoid involvement.

"Lie down and take it easy, dear," Mrs. Winner cooed. "You'll feel better after a little nap." She escorted Mrs. Carlisle up the stairs. Some strands of Mrs. Carlisle's auburn hair fell across her face, and a small decorative comb dangled at her neck. Her eyes settled into an unfocused stare and she moaned as if witness to a private vision. It happened so quickly to her, the transformation from exquisite and sublime to disheveled and deranged.

I caught up to them on the second floor. "Anything I can do to help?"

"Don't worry," Mrs. Winner assured me. "This is women's work."

Mrs. Carlisle covered her face with her hands. Then as her expression hardened, she turned on me and spat, "Don't you *ever* do what he does."

Mrs. Winner frowned toward me and jerked her head toward the stairs.

Wendy was filling the coffeepot at the sink. "Are you having a good time?" She slipped the pot onto the stove and lit the gas with a match.

"Mrs. Carlisle is falling apart. Your mother just took her upstairs."

Exactly on cue Mrs. Winner hurried into the kitchen and set about preparing tea for her patient. "She hadn't eaten. Drank her eggnog too fast. Such a shame. She's not bad. It's *him*." She nodded in my direction.

"Me?"

"Not you," Mrs. Winner said.

"He thinks he's the center of the universe," Wendy clarified.

The boiling water activated the women. Tea brewed and sandwiches were made with a flurry of fingers. "A shame," Mrs. Winner repeated as she scooped up the hasty meal and departed.

"She's got more wrong than missed meals." I said, making my voice as deep as possible to convey authority. "Mr. Carlisle never showed at Christmas. They said he was busy doing relief work. But there's no food in her house. I had to go out and do the shopping. He should bring relief to the starving Americans.

"She has these moods," I continued. "I mean, this morning I woke up and she was sitting on the coffee table right next to my couch all dressed, filing her nails. Like it was the most normal thing in the world. When I said hello, she looked at me like I was some sort of beast. I thought she was going to run that nail file up my nose. I dressed and went for a long walk."

"You have such an imagination," Wendy said. "I don't believe half of what you say. Half? I don't believe anything you say."

"She's got problems. And I all but begged her to take me home for the holiday."

"From what I hear, her husband is very unfaithful."

"He never showed. I took many walks around Zurich I

ended up with Abbott and Costello at the movies. 'Hey, Aa-but!'" I couldn't resist mimicking the call of Costello, then felt a fool in the midst of it.

Wendy crossed to fetch some cups from the cabinet behind me.

"She's a very nice person," I said. "Her husband must be driving her nuts." The scent of wildflowers beside me, her fluffy sweater leaving stray strands on my shirtsleeve. This is what I had been waiting for. I set the eggnog on the counter and ran my hands along the flare of her hips.

I kissed her fine puff of hair. "Let's go somewhere. Be alone."

"Hank, darling. I adore being with you. I really do." She sounded like she was repeating lines from a romance magazine.

"These past days with Ruthie and her mother seemed like forever," I said. "I dreamed of seeing you today. Here you are more beautiful than I imagined."

"You are so sweet." Her hand rested on the back of my neck.

Here I go. I know the rule: *Don't say it unless it's true.* But it's true all right. "Wendy. I love you."

"What?" She halted, stricken.

"I love you. I do."

"Oh, Hank. Don't say what you don't mean."

"But I do mean. I mean with all my heart."

The air seemed to leave her. She slipped away, head lowered.

"You don't have to say you love me," I covered in self-protection.

One of the guests ambled in, grinning. *"Vasser?"* he asked. Wendy filled a glass and thrust it at him. "Zank you." He downed it in one draft, raised his glass in a delayed toast and ambled out.

"This is going wrong," I lamented. Then I remembered and produced the little package from my pocket. "I bought you a fabulously expensive Christmas present. I was going to give this to you first, then recite the poem I wrote for you."

"Poem?"

"Sure. Did you write mine?"

"I was so busy." We both recognized a lie in the festive air.

"That's OK. Mine is bad enough for both of us."

"I thought you liked my poetry."

"I do. I can't resist the wise-guy remark."

"Like saying you love me."

"I meant that."

"How can I tell?" she asked.

"You're aware of when I'm kidding and when I'm not."

"Not always."

"I love being with you. Talking with you."

"Whenever we're together you make a serious pass at me."

"The night of your poem, you were doing the passing."

"Josh is right about you." She slapped a hand on the counter while a pent up cry rang from her.

"Josh?" The very sound of his name turned my insides. "What the hell has he got to do with us right now?"

"Nothing. I didn't mean to say his name."

"He puts these doubts in your head. What has he told you?"

"He doesn't tell me. We discuss things. He's brilliant. He can recite Byron and Shakespeare by the hour."

"With spit flying and throwing books at his listener."

"You boys drive him to that. Alone with me he's different."

"What's he do after the recitations?"

"Not what you do. He's a gentleman."

"The only physical contact he likes is with his own mother."

"I think," she began, "that is a very nasty thing to say." She didn't sound convinced that I was wrong, however. To keep busy, she washed the cups on the counter, both used and clean. Suddenly, she sobbed.

"Don't cry for the likes of the Brackbirns." I placed a tentative hand on her shoulder, afraid that my touch might cause her to flee. "They're weird. Lily is having an affair, if that's the word. Josh is a bull artist, believe me."

"How can I believe you? You're the one who does things to me. Then afterward you laugh at me. At the school. At everyone."

"I laugh at stupidities. I don't laugh at my feelings for you."

"Josh writes me beautiful letters. Tells me his most secret thoughts."

"He's taking advantage of you. You're his young student."

"I'm not so young. I'm sixteen."

"Fourteen."

"I'll be sixteen in two days."

"That's not what you've been telling me."

"I don't remember telling you my age, Mr. Smarty. Sixteen in two days. Josh and I celebrated the night before we left for the holidays. He's not that much older than me. Only three years. My father is *four* years older than my mother."

"You're talking about Josh like he's your husband-in-waiting."

"I'm simply saying."

"Josh is using you. If Lily were available—"

"You say anything that comes to mind, Hank. Half the

time I don't know what you really mean. All I know is that we always end up with your hands all over me. Josh says you're a bundle of hormones and Midwestern bluster wrapped for export."

"Boy, he's sure got me down cold."

"Always the flip remark."

"I don't snow girls with Byron and Shakespeare and pretend I don't want to love them. I'm a normal, growing boy."

"I'm a normal, growing girl. But I appreciate other things in life besides what your main interest is."

"My main interest is life. All of it. The people, the poetry, the skiing. Especially, the girl. That's you."

"Josh told me I'm his favorite. You only want me to get even with him."

"You believe him?"

"He says I should forget about you. You'll only hold me back."

"He's got no right to say that."

"He's a genius. He discusses Proust with me."

"I'll discuss Proust with you. What is it?"

Wendy fluttered her lips in exasperation. "It's *Who* is *he*? He's a great French Jewish writer."

"Not the Jewish thing. Did he bring that up?"

"He said that gentile guys, like you, have no permanent interest in Jewish girls like me. You play love games with us, then brag to your gentile buddies. He warned me to beware."

"What did you say to that?"

"He's so intelligent, it's difficult not to believe him."

"He thinks this gentile will love you and leave you. But what's he doing? Toying with you. A girl much too young for him. I don't care how you add it up. A nineteen-year-old guy is a lot older than a fifteen- or even a sixteen-year-old girl."

"He's so clever. He knows so much."

"The Jewish thing is nothing to me. Josh being Jewish doesn't make him a jerk. It's possible to be a jerk no matter what your race, color or creed."

Wendy half-closed her eyes and began describing what sounded like a visit with a deity. "When I'm alone with him, I'm transfixed. He recites poems and passages without opening a book. His eyes burn so brightly. If he touched me, I'd dissolve."

"In pleasure or fear?"

"I'm not sure." A light shone from her face as a great discovery illuminated her being. "The fact that he *doesn't* touch me enhances the spell. He's after my mind and nothing else. That makes him so hard to resist." The fanatical cast in her eyes stirred a profound unease in me. "Sometimes he scares me so, I have to cry. But he's so exciting. Oh, Hank." Her head dropped against me and she began to cry. "I don't know what to do."

"I know what to do."

The swell of her sweater brushed me. In a rush to embrace her, I jostled a glass into the sink, where it shattered.

"Broken glass," I said. "No one walk through this sink barefoot."

Wendy exhaled a deep, purging sigh-laugh and slapped my arm. She blew her nose and shook back her hair.

"Josh and I have a rivalry," I said. "We're both bigmouths and pigheaded. But that's not our problem, yours and mine. I'm happy as a swine in mire when I'm with you."

"A swine in mire?"

"I'm quoting Lord Byron. Or is it *Sir Gawain*?"

"You are such a nut." Her belittling tone lifted my heart. "I'd like to believe you. But when I'm with him, it's different." Her anxiety returned. "His power frightens me so."

"I'm gonna have a little heart-to-heart with Josh. Get him straightened out. He won't use you unfairly. I'll see to that."

"You will, too, if I know you."

"I'll have him eating wedges of Gerber cheese from the palm of my hand." I raised her chin. "Don't listen to anyone but me. That way you'll stay out of trouble." I smiled my cocky, king-of-the-hill, American smile.

"Josh says that too. You sound just like him."

"I'm nothing like him." I flapped my arms in despair. "Listen, next semester will be an all-time great one. The whole gang of us together."

"Next semester." She said it dreamily, a far-off event too distant to contemplate. I touched her wool-clad shoulder. "You want your fabulously expensive Christmas gift?"

She unwrapped the small package gingerly as if it might contain a stink bomb. Inside the shiny cardboard box, between two layers of white cotton, coiled a thin chain bracelet with a heart dangling from it. "It's beautiful," she said with as much feeling as I had hoped. She read aloud the inscription on the heart: "OB *aime* PK."

"It was on sale. I couldn't afford one with our initials. It's cheaper to change our names." A major gamble: Girls don't like to joke about a serious matter like jewelry. Wendy studied the bracelet for a long moment as she repeated the initials. "I'll be Peggy Kramer. Who are you?"

"Otto Bismarck."

She gripped me in a tight hug as I threw my long arms around her head, which nestled against my chest. I heard her cry again, and my eyes watered.

"Hank, I do care for you. Very much."

"It's Josh who's in our way. But I'll fix that. They didn't send me over here to lose the girl to a guy like him."

"You two be careful," Mrs. Winner called from the kitchen doorway. "Don't make a foolish mistake that would ruin your lives." We opened our embrace and Mrs. Winner slipped in. At the sight of our tears, she joined in. "Crying on the holidays."

"Tears of joy," I explained, hoping it was true.

THE SEA OF CLOUDS

Chapter Twenty

I left Zurich the next day. I had been there a week, although it seemed a lot longer. Ruthie had spent a lot of time gazing out the window and taking catnaps, even at the dining room table. We never fell into the playful banter we had enjoyed at school, even though I tried to get her going with my poor imitation of Monsieur Gillet broadcasting his coded messages. Mrs. Carlisle overdid her excuses for the absence of her husband and her performance at the Winner's party. She referred to both often, each time checking my reaction to see if I was buying her line. When I told her I had to leave for Paris, she seemed genuinely relieved. I would no longer be a witness to her disastrous holiday season.

She gave me a ride to the train station, where she shook my hand. "Have a good time in Paris," she said. Her face clouded and she added, "Don't think too badly of us."

"I don't. Really. Thanks for taking me in."

"The holidays aren't always a family's best time." She turned her head away as she heard that this excuse sounded no better than the others.

I made my way inside, but instead of going to Paris for the remainder of the holiday break, I found myself buying a ticket for Neuchâtel. There was business with Josh that I had to settle, the fire to confront him rekindled by my session with Wendy at her family party.

The train streaked across Switzerland, a ground-hugging bolt of lightning flashing along the basin of land among the mountains. I started to write my thoughts in a beat-up pocket notebook with a mechanical pencil I always carried, rehearsing for the day when I would be an ace reporter. The pages contained odd musings, such as key French phrases and vocabulary, *Cela va sans dire.*

Blinding insights into human nature: *People often say anything that comes into their heads, even when it has nothing to do with the current conversation.*

Or, *Josepina and Sylvana are like otters. They enter a room playing with each other, tickling or slapping in fun and soon have everyone laughing along with them.* Sylvana taught me a poem she made up about her friend:

"Signorina Josepina,
Collo gamba de gallina."

Check spellings in an Italian dictionary, I had written beside the poem.

It means, "Miss Josepina, with the legs of a hen." Sylvana points to her friend's skinny bowed legs. Josepina smiles, being a good sport. But she doesn't really like her legs being made fun of, particularly in front of a male. I see the hurt in her eyes and the way she tugs to make her skirt a fraction of an inch lower to hide her embarrassment.

A recipe for vegetable spaghetti sauce was written while I watched Josepina work her magic when I was still the only student in the school.

Josh and Wendy, I wrote. *An older male lording it over a younger female student. Lily and Dun. A headmistress plucking off the most manly student. What the hell kind of school are they running?*

I allowed my anger at Josh to build. I mulled and recounted, pushing myself to my special form of outrage, hostility close to irrationality centered on my nemesis. But as my urge for combat swelled, my gut relayed a familiar, undesired sensation. I felt sorry for the guy. This is spite of his outrageous pretensions. The time and effort he expended convincing the world of his brilliance.

His consuming desire to rule the world his mother had created for him with his missing father's mysterious bankroll.

I withered in the grip of this concern for that pathetic teenager who had shuttled from England to Chicago, escaping a war to be dropped among strangers. One year of college could not quell the desperate drive to be heard. But saying what and to whom? Impressionable girls and lost males unacceptable at any other institution of learning? It was all so petty and sad. I recalled Josh standing sentinel at the library door, his arms folded, repeating the advantages of a European education while his mother carried on with Dun. Was Josh a cuckold, or just a man standing guard for his mother? What memories could Josh summon of his missing father? Josh had the advantage of a comfortable life but no man to learn from or admire as I did.

My righteous indignation wavered. Vengeance proved elusive when you had even a shred of feeling for the enemy. To rekindle my wrath, I closed my eyes and pictured Josh braying, harassing and sneering at us. I imagined how he treated Wendy. He drew her into his confidence, quoted literary giants not to edify but to dominate her. Then when the young woman was in his thrall, he ridiculed my raw American enthusiasm and energy. The very American qualities that had rescued Europe.

Yes, that was the true Josh. A scheming manipulator who turned his perverse talents onto kids. But he had chosen the wrong kid to mess with. I would stand up for what was right. The hell with this sloppy holiday sentimentality and forgiveness. I knew how to fight back. I would battle for all my classmates, the ones Josh had humiliated, mocked and intellectually seduced. I burned with conviction. I vowed to cease stewing over the events that had led to this moment. It was time to act. Josh must be confronted at the school, our battleground, right now in the midst of the holiday break. We would settle our differences and start the new year with fresh resolve.

The funi glided up the mountain, the little car burning brightly on the slope. Where the single track bowed to allow its downward rolling twin to pass, I half expected to see someone from the school inside. Perhaps Josh in a tear. But no familiar faces peered from the other car. At the summit station the funi burst open with a clatter of sliding doors. The harsh blue overhead lights penetrated like X rays. I trotted up the frozen snow road to the school.

The château blended into the night, pitch black against the dark evergreen background. Not a lamp glowed, which was puzzling. Lily had told Mrs. Carlisle that they would be at the school, working over the holiday. Josh had probably gathered up all the bulbs lest someone have the audacity to desire light. They were there in the dark.

I trotted up the few steps to the terrace. The French doors of the dining room were closed, but barely. I didn't even have to turn the latch to push them open. Inside the cold confines of the cavernous dining room I could hear sounds like muffled crying. Originating from a distant section of the building, the forlorn notes drilled a chill deep into my being. I edged my way carefully past the long dining table and scattered chairs to the yawning stairwell. The wide wooden stairs creaked in the cold. I felt my way to the boys' dormitory. The crying grew louder, more plaintive.

When I flicked on the light switch, nothing happened. The bulb had not been replaced. I dropped my Val-a-Pak and groped to the hiding hole in the closet where I had hidden the pistol. The cold steel of the firearm reassured me. I loaded it before thrusting it into my belt, feeling both heroic and stupid.

I flipped the hall light switch but the hall, too, remained dark. The strange wails seemed to come from the maids' garret. The women were supposed to be home in Italy for the holidays, but one of them may be alone and ill. I paused in the blackened hallway. Here I was, poking around in the dead of night packing a pistol like a leftover from some third-rate movie. I should go to the inn and ask to sleep on a couch for the night. But the crying, moaning, whatever it was, exerted a magnetic pull. If someone were in trouble, I couldn't turn my back. No true American hero would do that.

I gulped in a deep swallow of cold air and edged up the narrow garret stairs toward the sound, goose bumps of fear rippling across my skin. Again I touched the handle of the pistol under my belt. Its heft both reinforced and terrified.

"Hey, it's me. Hank." My cracking voice echoed through the hall. I half expected Josh's taunting retort, "It's me, Hank, is it?" But none sounded. My hand lingered on the handle of the maids' room door for several long moments before turning it. "It's me."

The force of the rush slammed me back against the hallway wall, my head bouncing off the paneling. The impact sent a bolt of bright pain through my head and then my body. As I sank to the floor, my hands clutched my forehead. All thoughts of the gun or defense washed away in the stunning waves. From out there, away from the daze and disorientation, I heard the scrambling, the scurrying, the frantic clatter. A wild force had been turned loose from the attic.

Rolling over to my hands and knees, I coughed, the contraction causing the gun to dig into my upper groin. The stench from the maids' room wafted into the hall to assail my senses. The room smelled as if something dead had been left behind to rot.

Downstairs, a dog's bark registered like a rifle shot in the night. I fled from the smell. I couldn't investigate that without a light. Stumbling from the attic, I half-slid down the railing of the main stairs—a trick I had performed so many times I could do it in a daze. The dog continued to yap in the kitchen. I wasn't sure whether it had some wild thing cornered or the dog itself was the monster I had set loose.

Pancho whined, cried, circled at a trot. Then he howled his plea for food and hurled himself at the closed cupboard doors. In his mad search, Pancho brushed by me, almost knocking me over. I called the dog's name. Although the starving creature stopped briefly to wag his tail, he had more elemental concerns. I found some kitchen matches and lit one. Little remained on the shelves. The match expired in the draft whistling up from the cellar. Pancho bolted past me to scramble and half-fall down the stairs. I heard the snuffle and smacking as the dog wolfed down stored potatoes.

Upstairs in the boys' dorm, the blankets had been stripped from every bed. All the footlockers had been opened and rifled, one even tipped on its side. Mine was the only one that had gone untouched. This could have been an oversight by a burglar, or Josh setting me up as the looter. I lay down on my bare cot and curled up in my coat, pondering whether to continue exploring the house or to wait until the light of dawn. The contemplation produced the desired effect. I dozed off, the wind wailing lamentations in the window frames.

A snowstorm hit overnight; at dawn the fluff was piled high on the sills. Beyond, it swirled in tumultuous patterns, the wind agitating it into a dancing veil. I scanned the windows, half expecting Josh to burst in, tip over my cot and denounce me as a lazy, slug-a-bed foreigner. My body was so chilled that my feet and hands held little sensation. I was punchy from lack of sleep. I couldn't seem to focus on what had happened to the school and what was happening now. Pancho resumed his barks and whines below.

I started to investigate. Gillet's room showed nothing but

his stripped cot and stash of empty wine bottles. A couple of tattered paperbacks in French lay in disarray on his shelves. His closet gaped empty except for a torn shirt, which appeared left over from another period of history. This told me little, because Gillet rarely used his quarters. He spent most of his free time in his mountain hut transmitting his reports to the potentate of Zyron.

I climbed the attic stairs to the maids' room with great apprehension. The odor had abated somewhat, diluted by circulating air. At the landing, I extracted the pistol from my belt and flourished it as a talisman to ward off evil. I imagined myself a GI searching a German castle in quest of a cornered Nazi field general.

I slipped past the door ready for assault, finger tight on the trigger. But no one jumped me. No sound or alarm was raised. No dead body sprawled on the floor. The only artifacts in the small room were the two bare cots and a few scattered torn cheap stockings. I checked under the beds and in a listing armoire that was braced under one corner by a pair of old bricks. The source of the stink proved no real mystery. Messy piles of Pancho's frenzied evacuations dotted the floor. He had been locked in and abandoned, his water and feed bowl empty. The door and walls had been ripped and gouged by the animal's desperate digging for freedom. Only Josh would treat a pet this way, another affront he would answer for. I surveyed the cramped room and repeated by rote the phrase that had bonded the maids to the boys: "It's foggy today."

In the girls' room, Ruthie's possessions remained neatly in place. But Wendy had carted off most of her belongings; only her curtains and pillows and the frills around her table bore proof of her presence.

I saved the Brackbirns' quarters for last. I fully expected to find mother and son sitting up in their beds in their overcoats, cackling over the trick they had played. I rapped on the door and paused. Nothing. I knocked again, feeling like a complete jerk, the purpose of my mission obscured in the chaos of the past few hours. I returned the pistol to my belt and again experienced the odd sensation of false assurance and embarrassment.

I tried the handle. Locked. Good. That meant they had gone to Neuchâtel for a few days. They hadn't abandoned the place. But I wasn't convinced. I wrenched the handle harder. This time the door lurched open as I pushed. Now the anger surged. If Josh were sitting in his bed chuckling, I wouldn't bother with highly reasoned and eloquent arguments. I'd let him have it. Blast him in the big toe. If that didn't make him beg for forgiveness, maybe a slug in the calf or thigh. Josh must pay for his arrogant disregard for others. I pulled out the pistol, my hand trembling. I'm not afraid to use it, I told myself, hoping it were true.

The room was vacant; one closet door flung open, wire hangers littering the floor, bureau drawers open. Next door, Lily's room mirrored Josh's. A few stockings and random belts like so many dead snakes lay across the bed and coiled on the bare floor. I smelled their smells so familiar from those first days at the school—the whiff of aftershave, the lavender scent of Lily, the stale tobacco smoke—faint yet distinct. I was even more a part of their lives now, sharing the intimacy of their bedrooms. But this moment with their memory brought a sickening dawning: they had run out.

One closet door remained closed. Maybe Josh was hiding inside. That would be typical of him, pretending to leave, then jumping out with that superior smirk on his lips. Damn him to hell! He had toyed with us long enough. I gripped my pistol, grabbed the closet door and jerked it open. A form lurched toward me, its arms reaching toward my throat. As it wrapped around my face and shoulders, I could see Josh's face twisted in a hideous grimace, mocking, primed for attack. The form closed over my face, suffocating me in its fervid embrace. I fired the pistol, once, twice, five times.

In horror I lurched backward. On the floor at my feet was Josh's bathrobe, the one he was wearing the last time I saw him, standing with his mother at the rear door of the mansion as we drove off to Zurich.

Staring in confused panic at the bathrobe, I summoned the will to nudge it with my right foot. When it moved I shied away as if it were alive. In fact, I had experienced its life force; it had assaulted me, smothered me. I had seen the face of my antagonist clearly. He was there. But where was he now? The empty robe lay still on the cold boards, the scratch of its woolen embrace still playing on my cheeks, the bullet holes barely discernible in the dark fabric. Had Josh dissolved under my fusillade? Again, I poked at the bathrobe, and when it stirred I leapt back in raw fear. But there was nothing under it. I was alone with the once animated cloth in the creepy cold of the deserted school.

I had to get away from the haunted place, out into the cleansing snowfall. On the terrace, the unceasing wind churned the snow from cream to butter, its blizzard force lashing at my face and stinging my eyes. I slogged down the hill toward the one place where logic still held sway. I sucked in a breath full of snow. Be composed. I represent America. Be calm, be cool.

"*Bonjour, madame.*"

Madame Montraux widened her dark eyes as if viewing a ghost. "*M'sieur.*" She nodded, her eyes not meeting mine.

"*Quel temps.*"

"*Mais, oui. Une tempête de neige.*"

"*Avez-vous des lettres de Chicago?*"

She moved her hand toward the normal slot for the school mail, then redirected it in mid-air. She slid open the drawer under the counter and drew out a small bundle tied with a cord.

"*Avez-vous vu les Brackbirns?*"

"Not for a few days, since they left," she answered in her clear French.

I asked where they had gone.

"To England," she said.

"When do they return?"

The poor soul, apple-cheeked, perpetually cheerful, had met her match. She shifted her glance from floor to ceiling and along the shelves of the little post office—store seeking help anywhere. The melting snow on my jacket made it smell like wet sheep. My face flushed hot from the heat of the pot-bellied wood stove in the corner.

"*M'sieur. Ils sont partis.*"

I raised my eyebrows and nodded with an ironic European smile. Surely I was nothing if not worldly and wise. Life was replete with minor inconveniences, nothing that couldn't be taken in stride.

"They are gone, M'sieur. Left with all their possessions. Gone."

"How interesting," I said. "Gone. That goes without saying."

Madame's young daughter called from the back of the store where they lived. The woman, welcoming the interruption, rushed to her, babbling a mile a minute in grateful anger.

I toured the school again, not sure why. Maybe I'd find a note or a message written on the wall. Something. Anything. Standing in the dining room, staring out through the glass doors, the sun-parlor classroom was off to my right. The library, stripped of Josh's precious books, opened to the left.

I owned the school at last. I had won, the only surviving member. My feet were planted on the waxed tile floor, my pistol returned to my belt. The victor. The wind cried on the deserted battlefield. Outside, the snow swirls concealed the titanic Alps. The Sea of Clouds engulfed the château, with me its only survivor.

THE SEA OF CLOUDS

Chapter Twenty-One

At the inn, I persuaded the manager to rent me a cheap cot in a storeroom, a snug, warm place to escape the winter. The weather was more unpredictable than ever. First the blizzard arrived, then a mountain-style hurricane with soaking rains that washed away all the snow. Wicked winds had caused a power outage, which plunged Chaumont into darkness and put the funi out of business for several hours.

I wrote my father explaining my plight and awaited a reply with details of my passage home. Still, I experienced great trouble pulling myself away from the school. I regularly hiked up the road to wander through the empty château. In the boys' dormitory my footlocker remained as I had left it before the holiday. Tony's was empty from his premature departure, but Hermon's still had some of his clothes; a pair of dress shoes was nearby. Dun's locker had been stripped clean and tipped awkwardly, a deep indentation on its side as if kicked in a rage. Maybe Josh had stolen Dun's belongings, and then attacked his locker. Maybe Dun had taken all his stuff with him to Paris. He probably knew the school was closing, warned by Lily. Maybe he had tried to alert me by telling me to expect the unexpected. But he couldn't tell me outright. A sharp dagger of betrayal pierced me; Dun couldn't confide in me. He was more loyal to Lily. He had allied himself with the Brackbirns at the expense of Tony and our pledge of mutual support. I had believed our friendship deeper than that.

Often when alone in the dorm I would emit a howl of pain,

sometimes without warning. I cried out in confusion and anger, feeling double-crossed by Josh, Lily, even Dun, and by the Fates who had carried me to this remote mountaintop. And betrayed in some mysterious way by myself.

I carried bones from Madame Montraux's little butcher counter and left them for Pancho outside the door. But the dog had disappeared. I fantasized that he was living somewhere in the woods with the Brackbirns, hiding until I set sail for home. Then all three would emerge to continue the school year without me. "I wouldn't blame them if they did," I said to no one as I ambled through the deserted château. "I'll bet they don't offer a scholarship to a kid from Hillard next time." I laughed my ironic, goofy chuckle at myself, my predicament and the foolishness of mortals.

I returned to Josh's bedroom and skirted the woolen robe, still sprawled on the floor. I poked at it with a foot, treating it gingerly as if it might turn on me if aggravated. But it remained an inanimate swirl of cloth. I picked it up and fingered the bullet holes gingerly, as though they were personal wounds. I then returned it to the hook on the back of the closet door. To reenact the crime, I swung open the door and watched the robe dance. I pulled on the door harder and harder until the robe finally flew out toward me, its sleeves reaching for my throat. But I couldn't make it sail off the door and wrap itself around me as it had then. Nor could I come close to imagining the face of Josh in the terrifying grimace; the grimace that had prompted me to empty my pistol into the robe thinking it was he. Still afraid of the robe's effect on me, I hurried from the room and down the graceful stairs.

"M'sieur—"

I spun in surprise. The guy standing in the open front door looked very official. A tight overcoat and somber snap-brim hat framed the doughy, noncommittal face of a jaded servant of the people.

"Please to come."

Of course. The cops sent to haul me away. Toss me in jail or chain me to the wall of a Neuchâtel dungeon—that was a specialty of the old fortress town. Or maybe even rub me out, à la Tough Tony. Amazing that it hadn't happened sooner. The small black car whisked me down the mountain. My limited French was perfect for small talk with the laconic guardian of the peace and property. But my thoughts tumbled incoherently. What were they charging me with? Had I really shot Josh? Had he escaped to lodge a complaint after ordering Madame Montraux to tell me they had left?

The station house looked just like a mansion in a movie where a French nobleman seals his bitchy wife behind a wall then drags his sexy maid into the master bedroom. An officer with a bristling black mustache sat behind an ornate table talking to another man who looked familiar. As he turned, I recognized him. He was the Frenchman who one afternoon had given Dun and me a ride from town as he was driving to his summer place. What we suspected turned out to be correct. Our secret little house in the woods belonged to the only person neighborly enough to give us a lift.

"This gentleman owns a house near your school." The black-mustached officer spoke French slowly, all too understandably. "Some windows of this house have been shot out. Does m'sieur know anything of this?"

The relief of confessing settled over me, and my lips moved to clear my soul. The shot-out windows seemed as nothing compared with my willingness to empty my pistol into Josh. But the confession caught in my throat. I sputtered, and in this hesitation I saw the police officer grasp the truth. I coughed as if that was all that was troubling me. The policeman narrowed his eyes. "Does m'sieur have a gun?"

"Here? In Switzerland?"

"Yes, here in Switzerland."

The policeman stared me down for many long minutes, his face a scrutable mask. I would crack under his gaze, the way icicles break off under the glare of the spring sun. My tactic began as a simple averting of the eyes, but the policeman's persistence, fueled by his inner conviction, steeled me. The meeting became a contest of wills. My eyes locked on those of my interrogator. As guilty as I was, I wouldn't be broken. The staring contest seemed without resolution. Then the policeman spoke. "You're an American. Perhaps some form of reparation?"

"That is to say, money?"

"Yes. Reparation for the damage."

I slumped in the chair mulling my choices. Paying for the damage was right and proper. But slipping from my defiant mood proved difficult. Before I could respond, the Frenchman, who watched this tug-of-war with fascination, broke in. "It isn't fair to ask this boy to pay. There is no proof he did anything." My skill at appearing sincere had won over another adult.

We sipped coffee and conversed at a café, the Frenchman enunciating clearly for my benefit. The French government was a farce; anarchy and revolution loomed on the horizon. Inflation had made money worthless, and it seemed that the only winners would be the Communists, who were plotting to take over in the turmoil. I recalled the tortures I had endured to grasp a minimal command of the language. Now that I had it, the Frenchman was listing the obvious truths I knew before I had set sail. I hadn't learned French to listen to a Frenchman complain. My goal had been to speak better than Josh.

The Frenchman paid the bill and gave me a ride up the

THE SEA OF CLOUDS

mountain. At the inn we shook hands. In the brief silence I sensed what a traitor like the Nazi collaborator Quisling felt like. I had showered bullets in this man's house for no reason and when given a chance to make good, I had weaseled out. Then I had accepted coffee and a ride from the same guy. Even now I lacked the strength of character to admit and repent. Reading my mind, the Frenchman narrowed his eyes the way the grand inquisitor had at the police table, his face a study in sorrow and resignation. He had been overcome by the plight of the youthful student and gone soft. Now he saw that the American had enough money to stay at the inn and showed every manifestation of a guilty conscience. If only he had pressed me for the costs. But he accepted his fate with another Gallic shrug, dropped the car in gear and sped off.

I waved, but the driver didn't look back. Standing in the fresh snow, I realized I would never be held accountable for anything I had said or done—good or bad, right or wrong—during my few months on the mountain. No available witnesses. No authorities existed to judge me. I could return to Chicago clean, the triumphant American back from wowing them abroad.

Inside, I searched through my clothing and pulled out the pistol and box of ammunition. When I departed the police station, my inquisitor was far from satisfied. He might be one of those French-speaking cops who hound you into eternity for stealing a crust of bread. Best to dispose of the evidence before the cop made a late-night call with a search warrant.

Plunging through the frozen underbrush on the mountainside, I penetrated the woods to scratch and dig with a frozen branch at a spot not heavily covered with snow. After arduous effort, I scraped a hole deep enough to serve. The pistol and bullets clanked into it. I covered them with the clotted dirt and tamped it down. I jumped up and down on the spot until my feet ached. Hopping alone in the woods in the dead of winter, I did a painful dance over the weapon won in solemn arms negotiations.

On New Year's Eve I wandered through town alone and uninvolved. I drank some wine at a few bars and mouthed a few inanities to the locals in my brand of French. I even attempted to join a crowd of students, a couple of whom I heard speaking English. But my heart wasn't in it.

The funi station outside of town was closed and dark, the last run made, the car safely tucked in its resting place under the sheltering roof. I studied the station house for a moment, walked around to the back and pulled myself onto the tracks. I began the ascent, stepping from cross tie to cross tie, bent over, using my hands to steady myself. I advanced rapidly, taking care not to brush the thick, greasy cable that ran down the center of the tracks. Luckily, no severe weather had followed the mountain hurricane of Christmas so the funi trestle lacked ice and snow. The trip up constituted more than a good workout. It reaffirmed a ceremony that had bestowed meaning on our little band.

Near the summit, I squatted on the ties to view the small city. The distant lights danced in the cold night. Bulbs in the town tower etched the year: 1947. I was where I wished to be, above the tumult, still existing in the past, recalling the night Tony, Dun, Hermon and I had scaled the funi, something no man had ever done before. I emitted my worldly laugh, still a childish snort. "No one can take that from us," I said into the night. "We did it."

As I gazed at the tower in the town below, the number 7 in 1947 flickered and blacked out. Immediately, a lighted 8 replaced it: 1948. A new year. In a moment a weak cheer reached my ears. As I prepared to resume my ascent, I heard the brief blast of a carnival band.

THE SEA OF CLOUDS

Chapter Twenty-Two

Sitting on the funi tracks at midnight, I felt like a real-life Hemingway character. I was under a cold, starlit, winter night sky witnessing the end of one year and the start of another—one era passes, another begins, the sun also rises. But the trip back on the *De Grasse* was stormy and marked by bouts of seasickness, just the opposite of the sunny, exuberant, new-world awakening I experienced on the trip over. One day during a gale, I was sitting in a deck chair, wrapped in a blanket like a frail, older person, and ordered soup from a waiter. My only semblance to a Hemingway hero was that I had fought an odd war with an undeclared enemy and was returning home feeling maimed and less than triumphant.

In Chicago I stepped back into the world of my youth. Now my white socks stood out garishly below the cuffs of my outgrown Levi's, my shirt sleeves failing by inches to reach my wrists and my Val-a-Pak emblazoned with identifying stickers from trains and ocean liners. Then I saw them. First, my father's head appeared above the crowd on the train platform. Beside him stood my mother in her tan wool coat with high collar and matching floppy hat. But Peggy reached me first, darting and weaving through the excited masses. In no time, they surrounded me, laughing, talking, half crying and hugging. I was safe in the arms of my loving family.

After my months in the isolated Swiss château with its student body of six, the large rambling buildings of the Hillard School buzzing with student life and activity brought a spasm of panic to my heart. I shrank before the familiar edifice feeling like a scared new kid, carrying a fresh notebook and set of new pencils. My flannel shirt and corduroys, long enough to fit properly, were still stiff from the counters of Marshall Field. In the cafeteria the scents of coffee, black bread and honey from the Swiss mountaintop gave way to the sweet blandness of milk, white bread and cherry Jell-O. The diet I had grown up on now clamped my lips shut and closed down my appetite. The shock of this encounter proved so unexpected that I broke out in a cold sweat.

"This food," I said to Buddy Miller who sat stuffing his face.

"Yeah?"

"Is it always ... I mean, we ate this?"

"We're still eating it, jerk."

I was alone, among old friends who were wolfing down the staples of our youth. Like Josh Brackbirn before me, I was the refugee from the European conflicts, uncertain, out of my element. Besides the food, there was the language. I felt hesitant about the cadence and vernacular, which changes so quickly among teenagers. I had been absent for what seemed a generation. Also, there was my physical being. I had departed as a boy sure I would return as a man.

"Your voice *sounds* like it's changed." More than a note of doubt from the interrogator, King Smith, who sat beside me in study hall.

"Let's take him down to the shower and see what he's got." This from Terence Snee, a pudgy kid with rheumy eyes. How the hell had a creep like Snee gained such authority? Before I left, Snee was lucky to be asked to play baseball at recess. Now, his voice carried the timbre of a leader, and his carriage bore the certitude of a middle-aged businessman.

"Hands off!" I snarled in a gross overreaction to the horseplay.

"Hey, *big man*," Terence said recoiling in faked fear, mimicking the villainous whine of Richard Widmark, who, in *Kiss of Death*, tied a sickly woman to her wheelchair and pushed her down the stairs. "What's he afraid of? Got nothing to show us?"

"That's it. Nothing to show." I trusted the truth would disarm them. The awful fact was that on the brink of my 15th birthday I was still not there. At times of severe doubt, dark waves of speculation washed over me. This was my fate. Half-developed sexually for the rest of my life. Mature enough to semi-perform but not filled out enough for adult function. Perhaps I was to be an adolescent Hemingway prototype, a teenage Jake Barnes, marred in Europe to my lasting sexual detriment.

Meeting my former female friends did little to assuage my doubts. While I had grown taller and a bit wider, many of them had filled out to womanly proportions. Beside them I still seemed the grammar school kid with high hopes, not the secure young man whose experiences and hormones had transformed his body in Europe.

One of my favorites from dance class, Holly, a hefty, unsure girl who was often the object of snide remarks from the boys—taunts that drove me to defend and favor her—now walked and spoke with winning poise. She kissed my cheek and whispered, "Welcome back, voyager."

Holly wore a man-size class ring on a thick gold chain around her neck that she fingered as we chatted. The gesture demonstrated that Holly, who had begged me to think about her when I was overseas, wasn't staying home nights dreaming of me. The owner of the ring, a swarthy upperclassman with fleshy nose, ears and hands, each of which sported tufts of black hair, soon appeared wearing a crisp white letter sweater with the coveted blue *H* on the left side.

"Hey, how's it goin'?" He felt it incumbent to display his power with a crushing handshake. "How was Sweden?"

"Switzerland, Bernie," Holly corrected with a soft laugh.

"That's what I said," he answered, giving Holly a squeeze of ownership around her nipped waist.

"Isn't he something?" she asked me.

"He's something, all right."

Joy Moody presented a different but no more satisfying story. Unlike Holly, she hadn't exploded into female pulchritude. She continued to be the same slight girl with the silky voice and air of mild disorientation as if events spun by too rapidly for her to grasp—an older version of Ruthie Carlisle—a person I could be at ease with and talk to honestly without engaging in the poses and postures that more dynamic females prompted. But she received me in a casual way that denied the nervous electricity that had once crackled between us as boyfriend and girlfriend. Instead, Joy fumbled and fidgeted, backing off two steps for every one I advanced and often glancing over her shoulder as if expecting rescue. When I asked her out, she stalled, forcing me to withdraw the offer.

"Do you have a new boyfriend?"

"Not really."

"Then ... ?"

"We'll talk about it."

But we never did. My absence had rotated me out of her schedule. In high school, not being present at every social event proved ruinous.

Mike Straus greeted me warmly in the hallway outside of French class. "So you really tore it up over there?"

"Laid waste to everything *suisse*."

"I have to read in French today. Don't make me look bad."

"I couldn't if I wanted."

"We know."

Mike read from the text, his diction clear, his accent practiced. He spoke French as he did English, with conviction and in complete control. Yet he darted his eyes sideways toward me to recognize that I owned the experience to correct his efforts. At my turn came a rustle of anticipation. "Now we'll hear *French*," Mike assured the class. My insides flip-flopped as they had when Josh zeroed in on me. Razor slices of nervous sweat slid down my rib cage. I opened my mouth and squeaked. The class stirred and then tittered. I tried again but couldn't speak. They gathered around me in the hall.

"Whatsa matter? Scared to show us up?"

"Yeah. That's it."

"It was lousy over there, wasn't it?" The bass tones of Billy Curtis, the guy who knew it all from what not to promise women to the Jewish conspiracy, resounded above the clatter of the class change.

"Yeah, lousy." Then I caught myself. I wouldn't give in like that. "I mean, no. It wasn't that bad. I learned a lot."

"Cripes, Douglas. You look like you're gonna puke."

"Perhaps I shall."

"*Perhaps I shall!* " Billy mocked the arch phrase. "You with a bunch of pansies over there?"

"Europeans, jerk," I snapped.

"It stunk. I can tell by the way you're acting." Billy faced the rest of the gang. "I don't see no jealousy on these faces."

"I met some great people who were really swell to me."

"I remember Josh Brackbirn when he was here. He was a turd. Tell the truth, the Brackbirns were shits, weren't they?"

"The Brackbirns." The memory of Josh returned to taunt me. The sneer. The superiority. The competition for power and for Wendy. The maltreatment of Pancho. The abandonment of the school. The consuming anger that allowed me to squeeze off rounds of lead into his robe believing it was he. With great deliberation, as if I had given the matter much weighty thought, I said, "The Brackbirns were a couple of kikes."

"What?" Billy Curtis exploded with glee.

Someone in the group clapped and cried, "I knew it!"

Billy burst from the pack and grabbed Mike Straus, who was passing by. "Tell him what you just said about the Brackbirns," Billy demanded.

I faced Mike and repeated, "The Brackbirns were a couple of kikes."

Mike Straus gave a muted huff as if someone had punched him in the stomach and then turned on his heel and walked away. If I had plugged him in the gut with Tough Tony's pistol, he couldn't have looked more surprised or wounded.

"So you *did* learn something over there after all," Billy Curtis crowed. When he slapped me on the shoulder, I bolted for the boys' room to hang over the toilet waiting for the purge. I ran a finger down my throat. I gagged and coughed but the release did not come. I doubted that it ever would.

That night I grabbed the familiar bus to Mike's house. The limestone front glowed in the night, the wrought-iron doorway as inviting as ever. Doc answered the bell, a woman's nylon stocking over his pomaded hair like a skullcap to preserve his konk. Nothing here had changed.

"You back."

I shook hands and half-hugged the mentor of our youth.

"How was that French nookie?" Doc asked.

"Best in the world."

"Don't I know."
"It's really great to see you, Doc. Really great."
"Yeah," Doc agreed. "Wanna eat?"
"I ate at home."
"He's up in his room." Doc nodded toward the curving stairway. "I expect you know the way."

Mike slouched on his bed reading. The first thing I noticed was the small basket over the closet door for the indoor games. We used the special little ball, a canvas cover with a rubber bladder we blew up like a balloon.

"Whatcha reading?"
"*Hiroshima*. For Current Events."
"Over there I read Molière plays in the original French."
"We're reading him in French class."
"He's funny, don't you think?"
"Yeah. What else you read over there?"
"*King Lear.*"
"We're reading Shaw's *Pygmalion.*"

"Mike." Now was the moment. Confess my confusion, my inability to think straight since my return. I tried but it came out oddly. "It wasn't right over there."

"Yeah?" Mike waited to hear more. But I felt the very power of speech leave me. My time to be eloquent dissolved into a painful period of awkward silence. I walked around the room, pretended to make a lay-up in the little basket and sat on the edge of a chair. Gradually, I found a small voice. "I fell in love with a girl over there. Girl from Long Island, New York. Jewish. Real smart. Hot too."

"Jewish girls are smart and hot. That's what they say."

I wasn't accustomed to this tone. "Mike." Again he waited. Again I felt my throat constrict, the correct words that had been so readily available all my life now locked and imprisoned in some secret dark dungeon of my being.

Mike lowered his book and gazed at the little rim.

"We had some wild games here," I tried.

"Still do," Mike answered.

We didn't say much more, some bits of gossip, forced and without warmth. Before I left I prepared to extend my hand toward my old friend, but either Mike sensed it coming and recoiled, or I drew back in fear of being rejected. Or something else. Or all of those things. The reconciliation, the object of my trip to see him, was not made. It should have been so easy. A few simple words. An honest expression of regret. But the easiest thing didn't happen.

"I'll see you tomorrow," I said.

"Yeah," Mike agreed.

I checked one last time. I hoped the pain in Mike's eyes was from *Hiroshima*. But I knew better.

In my room I flopped in the chair at my desk and stared at the wall. Before me hung a painting of the *Flying Cloud*, a square-rigged China clipper, under full sail, knifing through a choppy blue sea. Near it, a group portrait of the 1945 Chicago Cubs, the team that took the World Series to seven games before falling in a heart-rending defeat to the Detroit Tigers. Overhead, tilted above me on thread tethers, flew the model warplanes of my boyhood. A B-17 Flying Fortress and a B-24 Liberator, bombers bristling with protective machine guns. Providing cover on their flanks hovered fighters, a P-51 Mustang and a twin-tailed Lockheed P-38 Lightning. The frail little planes and the musty pictures on the wall seemed mementos of a distant time.

I had often wondered how I would react when it was my turn to serve in the armed forces. Would I go ready to kill or be killed for those back home? Or would I hang back, seeking refuge in a trumped-up deferment? Now, I couldn't imagine myself in the march of heroes. Today I had made a vicious racial jibe not once but twice, the second time deliberately to hurt my best friend. I went overseas bearing the pride of my country, school and family. I returned to spit out a hateful cliché, one favored by the weak and jealous, the ignorant and the cowardly. Then I had frozen when it came time to say I was sorry.

With a wild, undirected upward swing, my hand glanced off two of the planes at the lowest level, sending them dancing on their threads. "Slacker!" I hissed. I'd have been a slacker, a draft dodger, begging to be spared like the jerks in the war movies who didn't have the stuff to answer the call.

I swung again. This time the Flying Fortress bounced as though hit by enemy flak, a thread snapping from the force, leaving the plane listing at an undignified angle. I stared at the teetering model and debated whether I should punch it to seal its fate. Instead I watched, dumb and glassy-eyed.

Chapter Twenty-Three

"Every vegetable available," I gushed, hoping enthusiasm would offset a lack of cooking skills. "Throw them in with the sautéed ground round, then the tomato sauce. Stir it up as it cooks. The trick is not to overcook the spaghetti." I lectured the family as I bent over the pots on the stove, demonstrating the simple menu Josepina had taught me.

"Josepina made this look so easy," I said as I prodded and poked at the ingredients in the pots. "Mine doesn't smell as good as hers."

"It smells wonderful," my mother said.

"Just like a European dish," my father tried.

"I smell something burning," Peggy said.

"Those are the onions," my mother said.

"The hell they are," Peggy shot back. "I know onions. This is burning."

"Let's watch our language, young lady," my father said, unable to contain a smile. Peggy's bluster always reached him.

"She's right. The flame's too high." I scraped the wooden spoon across the pan where it met the resistance of the overheated vegetables.

"Turn it down," Peggy ordered.

"It's burned, ruined."

"Just singed. It'll be fine," my mother allowed.

"This never happened with Josepina."

"She's done it all her life. You're just starting. It smells wonderful."

"I hope we don't die from the carbon," Peggy said.

"This isn't burnt and you won't die," my father announced.

"I'll just have butter on my spaghetti," my sister said.

"You'll have Hank's sauce and like it." My father sounded gruffer than he had intended. "He's showing us what it was like over there. We can all learn from it."

Peggy moaned dramatically and said, "I'll update my will after dinner."

The so-called French bread that I had bought at the supermarket was spongy white bread in the shape of a baguette. The spaghetti and vegetable sauce resembled a meal from a can, not the work of a savvy European chef.

"It needs some spice," I suggested.

"Not for me, my mouth's on fire." Peggy waved her hand in front of her face with great exaggeration. "It's good," she added with surprise.

"Delicious," my mother agreed. "I can tell from the way you prepared this meal that you had some good times over there." She was still trying to convince herself.

"I met some great people. Anthony Joseph Heath-Merriweather. A real case. He could imitate Josh. I defended him until we found a picture of Hitler in his trunk."

"Hitler?" my father asked.

"He was one of those English aristocrats who thought Hitler might bring stability. I fought him about it."

The table fell silent. It was Sunday evening at our new house in a small town in New Jersey, well outside New York City. Pop had one of his few days off. He was working long hours at his new job, establishing himself at the *Times*. The meal was an attempt to get me to tell about my months abroad, a subject I had refused to discuss back in Chicago. Now we were a family thrown together in exurbia with no set of friends, far from the land where we had spent our lives.

"You wrote about your friend Dun," my mother tried.

"Yeah. Dun. He looked like a French Resistance fighter. But he wasn't."

"I should think not with the war over," she said.

"He collaborated."

"What?"

"Nothing. He was all right. He couldn't help it."

"Help what?"

"Nothing."

"Well, this meal certainly shows you got plenty from your trip," Mother said, then added, "I hope I'm drawing the proper conclusions."

The meal brought on thoughts of the Italian maids. "It's foggy today."

"What's that?"

"Something Hermon taught the maids."

"Really? Tell us."

As in French class at Hillard, my jaws locked. I couldn't speak a word.

"Tell us, Hank," my father added. In the silence, my mother shot a long, worried look at her husband.

Peggy reached over and held the hand in which my fork was poised. "I'll tell about my jerky French teacher if you'll tell about yours." Her assertive tone, full of teenage brio, brought laughter to the gloomy table, far more than the remark deserved, thanks to the circumstances.

After dinner we did the dishes while Pop made fudge, his favorite Sunday endeavor. The smell of cooking chocolate wafted me back to my younger days in Chicago, standing by the bubbling pot and recounting my adventures at Hillard to my parents. Then my father would tell about the war in Europe, the campaigns and strategies, the bombing raids and troop landings and battles. Imagine feeling nostalgic for a war. But it was my time of promise and dreams, a time that had receded into history.

With the dishes done, I drifted to my room, still not sure of its location in the new house.

"The fudge is almost ready," I heard my mother call.

"I'll be right out."

I sprawled on my bed in the gathering dark to stare at the ceiling. When my father was offered a better job in New York, he feared I would be disappointed to leave. But I was ecstatic. Here was a chance to break away from Chicago and Hillard; a place to start over. Peggy had her own reaction. "Oh my God," she moaned. "Leave Hillard? I'd rather die. I'll take a warm bath and open a vein and end it peacefully." Turning on me, she added with great flair, "You're agreeing to move? How could you?"

"It's not healthy to go to the same school all your life."

My father tried to placate her. "Peggy, if you'd like to finish the school year in Chicago maybe we can work something out."

"Stay with friends like an orphan. Board me out like an animal, an unwanted stray." Her hyperbole got everyone smiling and united behind the move. We all knew this job was too great a break for Pop to refuse. We were going, period.

Even before we left Chicago I dropped out of Hillard. I said I was sick. I was sick all right, sick of myself in that school, sick of the humiliating French class where I stammered and sputtered. Sick of locker-room trials, concealing my physical immaturity by refusing showers and dressing in dark corners.

I had loathed my behavior around Mike Strauss as I beamed like a failed salesman praying that with overstated good fellowship, the foul epithet I had uttered might somehow be erased. But we both knew it formed an impenetrable barrier between us. I was alone, at a painful remove from Mike and his friends, unwilling to join the gentile gang led by Billy Curtis. I didn't aid my standing by remaining aloof; my preoccupation with Switzerland was interpreted as moody superiority by my peers.

During that time I stayed home and even started working on a model airplane. The kit of a DC4, the smell of Testors airplane glue, the exciting feel of my beloved X-acto knives comforting in its familiarity. But no sooner had I unrolled the plans on my desk and cut out the first pieces than I had lost interest. I couldn't take my eyes off the model warplanes dangling overhead, still at rakish angles on broken tethers from my slashing attack. Reminders of what I had said that day at Hillard.

Now, after dinner at our new house, I heard the light tapping on the door. "Come on in, Pop."

"It's so dark in here." He stumbled against one of the cartons and gave a small cry. "Walking around these boxes should be an Olympic event."

"I hear it will be in '52."

"Mind if I sit down?"

"Mind if I sit up?" I rose up on my bed, my eyes blinking purple dots in the gloom.

"Hank." Intimate talks plummeted the man into agony. He was a guy who rolled up his sleeves and did things. Edited difficult stories. Laid out the front page. Made snap decisions. Had zero tolerance for obfuscation, delay or verbiage. Discussing intricate personal matters with his son, be it the birds and the bees or some mysterious psychological ailment contracted in Europe, was not comfortable territory. No one grasped that better than I.

"It's OK, Pop. Don't worry."

"But I do worry. You haven't been yourself since you came back."

"Maybe this is myself."

"I know you. This isn't you." His simple statement of understanding and support shot tears to my eyes. "Hank, did something happen over there?" I didn't respond. "Did anyone hurt you in any way? You said one of your friends was a Nazi. Did he assault you in any way?" I couldn't speak. "It wouldn't have to be a fistfight. There are other ways. Did he touch you? Did Josh Brackbirn?" The man was near tears himself. His empathy filled the dark room. But I found it impossible to respond, to assure him, because I still felt the lingering injuries without being able to express them. "Hank, if anyone hurt you, I'll ... You're not alone."

"I know, Pop."

"Tell me what happened."

I spun on the bed to face the wall as much as I could. "I don't know."

"The Brackbirns were irresponsible, abandoning you like that. I should have done better research on them, not taken Dr. Brown's word. I didn't do right by you."

"No!" I couldn't allow my father to shoulder the blame. "Not you. Me." Although I clenched my fists and was almost biting my tongue in half, I became convulsed in tears.

My father dropped onto the bed beside me and put a protective arm around me, the arm that had always been there to shield me from unsuspected attack, the arm that hadn't been in Europe with me. "Cry it out, Hank. Cry it out."

We crouched in the darkened room among the packaged mementos of another time and place, while my sobs worked their passage through me.

"Do you want to talk to somebody? A doctor who might help?"

"I'm not that far around the bend, Pop."

"No one's saying you are. But it might help to talk to someone outside the family. You think it might?" He strove to sound sensible and understanding. But at that time seeing a psychiatrist was extreme. My father's tone reflected this ambivalence; he yearned to help me, but I knew from his question that he hoped my answer would be no. He hadn't sent his son to Europe to have him return so disturbed that he required professional attention.

"I'm OK."

"If you change your mind and want to talk to a doctor, or to me, I'll be glad to listen."

"I know, Pop." I heaved a sigh and ran my hands over my face, which was damp with tears. "I'm sorry, Pop."

"For what?"

"Everything."

"You have absolutely nothing to be sorry about. Your Mom and I are proud of you. You understand?" When I was slow to respond, he repeated it. "Understand?"

"Yep."

"Don't you ever doubt that."

But I did doubt it. They were uninformed. They didn't know what I had done over there and what I had said when I came back to Hillard. If they had known, they would have been hurt, disappointed, less forgiving. If I had my way, they'd never know.

"Let's have some fudge," my father suggested. The phrase rang so brainlessly folksy—fudge will fix everything—that we both laughed. "I sound like a damn fool."

"Yeah, you do," I agreed.

"Well, we both suspected I was all along, didn't we?"

But I didn't agree to that. Instead, I threw my arms around him and hung on in the dark. Out of habit, my father raised his arm to ward off my imagined demons.

We had moved during the school year. Despite all her protestations, Peggy plunged right into the local public school and seldom mentioned Hillard. But I had had enough school for that year. I decided to wait until fall and start over in sophomore year as if the time abroad had never happened.

During the day, I worked as a caddy at the country club. This simple physical labor calmed my mind. But at night, my situation began to define itself with brutal clarity. Europe had exposed me for the fraud I was. I went over as the star pitchman of myself and came back believing I had sold a false product. Promise without fulfillment. The glittering cloak of European culture, rather than add panache and style to my American persona, oppressed with the weight of unrealized expectations. I could always fool grownups into believing I was mature. But when it was time to stop talking and start being a responsible adult, I turned out to be a petty, mean kid shielding himself behind a racial epithet.

To get to work, I bought a snappy English motorbike on the installment plan. The peppy little Royal Enfield 125 cc, shiny black with silver trim, purred beneath me, its two-cycle engine humming. On the metal crest mounted on the front fender, glue-on silver letters spelled out my golf course nickname, "Chicago." The breeze rushed against my face and hair. The New Jersey countryside rolled by, farmlands still resisting the tide of tract developments. Only a scattering of houses stood among the working farms with fields of corn, potatoes and onions.

I twisted the accelerator on the handlebar and took the machine up to 60. The faster the better; the more the wind blew, the better the chance of leaving it all behind. The air crashed into me. I gave it more gas and leaned forward over the handlebars. "Gotta keep movin'. Gotta get away. Let's go, go, go!" I howled like a trapped animal.

A beat-up Ford driven by a line worker late for his shift at a nearby assembly plant cut a quick left across my path. The little motorbike glanced off the right front fender, sending me hurtling headfirst onto the curb. My skull cracked, forcing a bone fragment against my brain, and my left collarbone snapped. Witnesses said the sound that rose from me resembled the lonely wail of a siren.

THE SEA OF CLOUDS

Chapter Twenty-Four

I lay pinned to the hospital bed, my left shoulder weighted down with a sandbag to stabilize the broken clavicle, massive ice packs resting against my bloated head. The melt from the packs, the sweat from the summer heat and the fevers from an intermittent coma drenched me. The headaches and impaired vision induced panic as the world split into multiple images riding waves of dizziness and nausea.

The nurses and doctors soothed me forcefully by placing damp gauze in my mouth and tying my wrists to the bedsides with strips of cloth to limit motion. But the pain was inescapable. Thrashing my head from side to side to shake it loose sent bolts of agony crashing through my eyes. I begged the doctors for relief. I envisioned a life of blinding pain and triple vision, lashed to a bed while packed in ice. I'd groan to anyone who'd listen, particularly the doctor. "I'm like those poor kids paralyzed from polio. In an iron lung for life. Prisoners of the machines built to save them."

"You're not in that bad shape."

"Wanna trade places?"

The doctors finally gave in, as much to shut me up as anything. They had been waiting for nature do the healing, but nature wasn't cooperating fast enough, so a decompression operation was scheduled, despite the risks.

"What exactly did they do?" I asked an intern who had assisted at the operation. I lay in bed tranquil at last, sure I was on the road to recovery. A young man with a somber mien, he lit up at my question, glad to expound.

"Frontal X rays showed that part of the displaced bone had caved in to press against the brain, which caused the swelling. You knew that. The decompression procedure meant cutting away the offending portion of bone and leaving a hole in the skull. This accommodated the brain in its current state of enlargement and eliminated the pressure. Got it so far?"

"So far."

"The complications included avoiding a major artery—the middle meningeal—that travels past the afflicted area. Also, the dura, the membrane that wraps the brain, couldn't be scarred without increasing the risk of epilepsy."

"Epilepsy?"

"Sometimes an unwelcome by-product." His dark eyebrows linked over his nose in a solemn frown. He explained how the surgeon shaved the left side of the skull, then sliced a half-moon incision above the ear and pealed back the skin to expose the skull. He cut away a piece of skull bone and lifted it free. The area beneath came up clean, no rips, tears or lacerations to the dura or any of the vessel. The hole wasn't large enough to need a protective plate. The flap of skin was sewn back. In time the skull would heal itself as a layer of soft tissue hardens into new bone covering the hole.

"You'll keep that sickle scar as a battle souvenir."

"God bless whatever you did," I said. "No more headaches. No triple vision. It's almost like being alive."

The intern gave a quick smile and squeezed my good arm. "You'll be up and around in no time. Ready for school and homework." He laughed at his remark and started toward the door.

I called out to him. "Doc!" He paused. "I brought this on. The accident."

"How's that?"

"It was payback."

"For what?"

"Things I did."

"Nonsense. Accidents happen."

"When you deserve them."

"Don't punish yourself with half-baked Freud. A car hit you. Period. The ER is full of people in trouble. Are they all being punished?"

"Maybe not them."

"But you are. Sure, perfect logic." He took a half step back toward my bed. "Don't think that way. It doesn't do you any good." He twisted his stethoscope in his hands, uncomfortable at hearing a boy pass such harsh judgments on himself.

"Forget I said anything."

"Would you like to talk to someone? Someone in the field?"

"No. I'm fine now."

He gave me his most suspicious appraisal. "There is no physical retribution for personal actions."

"Don't worry. I won't throw myself in front of a car if I forget to walk the dog."

He took another step toward me and leaned forward. "You mustn't believe that life evens out imagined misdeeds with traumas."

"I didn't really mean it. Just said it."

"OK." He touched my good shoulder in a sign of solidarity, shot me one last worried look and hurried from the room.

In spite of my demurrals, I believed that I had sought out the accident. Nor did it bother me that it had occurred. It helped even the scales that balanced in my brain. My only mistake had been to reveal my thoughts to a doctor.

Almost unnoticed at the hospital was the completion of another physical transformation. Puberty had finished its long and tortuous workings. My voice ceased its uncertain breaks and trills. At least in body, I emerged as a full-fledged adult male.

But the retribution of the accident and advent of physical manhood didn't end the times of uneasy reflection. Sharp-toothed creatures from the recent past returned to eat at me as I tried to lose myself in the soft muffle of the bedside radio.

THE SEA OF CLOUDS

Chapter Twenty-Five

The road was narrower, the air not as clean as I remembered. The mist billowed under the spires of the Alps, but the mountains didn't seem as far away. A police car angled toward the observation tower near the funi terminal. An official yellow ribbon with a printed warning barred entrance to the tower ramp.

The school building still nested in the evergreens on the side of the mountain, its terrace open to the world. The château appeared empty, with a couple of torn shades at odd angles in upstairs windows and tufts of weeds sprouting from the masonry terrace wall.

I parked the little rattletrap of a car and strolled across an unmowed lawn rife with crabgrass and dead spots of tan blight. I half expected Josh to materialize on the terrace and order me inside for a lesson in great English literature. I almost stumbled over the sign driven into the ground: *à vendre*.

I braced for a wave of anguish and regret. I had arrived here as a student some fifteen years earlier. But at times the memories, often painful or unsettling, were as immediate as the present. The site was ingrained in me, as pertinent as one of my organs. I didn't tremble in its presence, however. I observed with studied dispatch as I might a browning photograph. Instead of the sharp commands of Josh, I heard the laughter of my friends as we waited for Monsieur Montraux and mail call. A calm settled over me as I surveyed the fairytale building. I took a deep purging breath and gave my worldly laugh, which once again burst out as a childish snort.

The door still tinkled when opened and the pot-bellied wood stove still smoldered in the corner. There were wisps of gray in the woman's dark hair but otherwise she hadn't aged, except that her face was even ruddier.

"*Avez-vous des lettres de Chicago?*"

She looked up, cocked her head to one side to better focus on the speaker, then brought her hands to her face. "My God! I know you!"

From habit, her French rolled gently, as if to a pet creature. To my surprise I understood most of it, better than at any time since I gave up on the language when I was in college. In answer to her questions I spoke in simple phrases like a child, all in the present tense and with elaborate hand-arm accompaniment. "Work as newspaper reporter. Small city in New England. My father dies in spring. I leave newspaper. Hitchhike around Europe. Buy very old *quatre chevaux*. Now drive to Spain. Maybe to write. I never see anyone from the school again. I try to contact Wendy, but I don't find her."

"Do you remember little Ruth, the American?"

I remembered all right.

"Well, she returned a few months ago. She wore long hair and beads and had a boyfriend with a beard who needed many baths."

"Of course. And the others?"

"Never a word."

"The Brackbirns?" My voice broke, an echo of my physical status then.

"We never saw them again."

"Pancho?"

"He turned wild in the woods. Attacked the sheep and the deer. M'sieur Montraux had to shoot him."

"Like me. Wild in the woods."

"You?" she laughed. "Never you."

"The school?"

"A French couple ran a school again, but it failed. Then it was a sanitarium for children with tuberculosis. But that was a while ago." She shrugged. "It's for sale. Are you interested?"

Hearing her suggestion crystallized what had captured my thoughts when I saw the sign on the lawn. Buy the school. Own it outright. No petty power conflicts with the proprietor this time. The school would be mine. The possibilities engulfed me in a hot wave of excitement. Hell, why not? I had some money saved, and my father had left me a small amount. I could swing it. This was the answer I was searching for. I had felt low and lost since my father died. I could settle down here. Really learn French and ski. Tie up those rasping loose ends that rubbed for half of my years on earth. The idea asserted itself as probable, almost inevitable.

"How much?"

"Very dear. That's why they can't sell it. The owners," she wiggled her hands in a dismissive manner. "Germans."

What's "very dear?" To her, a shopkeeper in a Swiss hill hamlet, a reasonable sum would seem a fortune. But to an American, the inheritors of the modern world, the sum might be pocket change. I took a few steps to stare out the shop window toward the road that led to the school. With a rush of anticipation I thought, This is why I came back. This is what the Fates have planned for me.

"Do you know a figure?" I asked.

She rattled off a number so quickly that I was left glassy-eyed. Responding to my confusion, Madame Montraux wrote the number on a scratch pad. Sure enough, the price was very dear, even to an unemployed American newspaperman.

I exhaled as though just awakening. As it had so often,

reality clubbed my extravagant romantic aspirations into submission. The pittance I was traveling on couldn't pay the heating bills at the château. How would I live? Run a school for throwaway kids?

"Only a dream," I said.

"Maybe someday," Madame offered as a sop.

A tall young woman in high heels, her hair up in a fashionable beehive, emerged through the curtains in the back of the store. Almond-shaped eyes highlighted her oval face. Her clothes were chic, her long nails perfect, her expression warm and familiar.

"You remember my little one, Claudine?" Madame beamed.

"Not like this."

"She was just a little girl then."

We shook hands. Her perfume, her milky skin, something reminded me of whom? God, it was Wendy.

"I heard you speaking," she said. "You remember your French."

"Simple phrases." I couldn't rid my voice of the thin, high quality, the tenor of my time here. "It is difficult for me to speak."

"But why?"

"Too much thinking maybe." I gave my version of the Gallic shrug.

"I'm going to Florence to study Italian. It will be my fourth language. We Swiss must speak many languages, you know. I leave in a few days."

I couldn't take my eyes off her. She stepped forward from the past, a vision from that time of searching and turmoil.

"Are you driving to Neuchâtel?" the mother asked. "She must shop."

As I said my goodbyes, I asked about the police car and warning ribbon at the observation tower.

"Very sad," Madame said. "Yesterday a man jumped."

"Killed himself." Claudine twisted her fists in opposite directions as if wringing a chicken's neck.

"My God." I was unsure of the symbolism of the event, coming as it did on the eve of my return. "Life is difficult on this mountain."

Taking this as a compliment, the women nodded in agreement.

Claudine's presence filled the tiny car. How barren it had been before she occupied the front seat. As I eyed my passenger, a rush to share with her my moment of release at the château overcame me. I began in English, rapid-fire, words flowing.

"In my weakest moments, I imagined that the château was a proving ground where I had failed. I did stupid things there. Me, the pick of my Chicago school." I emitted a laugh of self-derision. Claudine displayed an edge of apprehension at my frantic tone. One hand gripped her door handle for a hurried emergency exit. I noticed but couldn't stop to reassure her.

"I was there to learn and grow and be made wise in Continental ways. But I got involved in school politics and love affairs. Defended a Nazi. Shot up a friendly neighbor's house. When confronted, I denied it. I thought I'd shot Josh. Then I went home to insult my best buddy." I paused for breath. "That's what's gnawed at me all these years."

I wasn't sure she understood. Her hand remained on the door handle, but her incipient panic passed. "I'm sorry I'm talking English and speaking so fast. Please forgive me."

"There is nothing to forgive," she said in perfect English.

"My first trip back. A lot of emotion."

"As I hear."

"Today I stood on the lawn, looked at the château and was at peace. I even understood French when you and your mother spoke. A minor miracle. I'm not sure I know what happened today. I was on my way to Spain. I was afraid to come here. Too many memories. But something drew me back, and I'm glad it did."

After a few moments I added, "You must think me a crazy American. Well, I was. Maybe I still am."

"I understand. You were a young man here. Young men make mistakes. You are difficult with yourself. Is that the right expression?"

"Exactly right."

"As you grow older, you must forgive yourself."

"You're right. Of course."

My brain shifted into overdrive. I couldn't let this wonderful human walk away. In my mind I struggled to say the right things: Do you have to go to Italy? I could stay in Neuchâtel. We could go out to dinner. Talk. Who knows? I'm single, uncommitted. My entire life awaits.

"How long do you stay in Switzerland?" she asked.

"That depends." My phony coyness rang hollow.

"It must be nice to be free. I have schedules and few holidays. My boyfriend wants to marry me before I travel to Italy. He thinks the Italian men will love me too much."

"He's right." I sounded so blunt. But a soothing relief swept through me. I couldn't invest any more emotion in people from that mountain. I sized her up again. She didn't remotely look or speak like Wendy. The resemblance when I first saw her had been a trick of memory. Yet even aware that it was futile and silly, I longed to pull the car onto the shoulder and enfold Claudine in my arms. In understanding and compassion. Something to show that I had come to grips with the past and would leave affection as my legacy.

But I remained locked behind the wheel. I feared that any embrace would be misunderstood as a physical advance. I lacked the vocabulary even in English to explain the subtleties to her. Maybe there were none. Maybe I simply desired to hold a beautiful young woman from the past, as a lover wishes to cling to a memory.

I kept my eyes on the road, the road that Dun and I, sometimes with Tony and Hermon, had walked so many times. Past the rock where we stopped for a smoke, under the trees that half-sheltered us from the rain.

In town she slipped out of the car and reached through the window to shake my hand. She had the no-nonsense grip of a person who knew where she was going. "I hope we meet again," she said.

"Me too. Good luck in Florence."

"I hope you find what you are looking for."

She had me pegged. In spite of my fancy talk in the car, to the practical Swiss I was still a lost soul. A grown-up kid from Chicago wondering what in the world had happened to him back then. Yet I felt a satisfying sense of completion as the European experience came to rest in my heart.

A light rain started to fall through the fumes of hundreds of little cars fighting each other for space in the streets. I edged the vehicle into the sluggish stream of traffic, a street where once we had strolled mindful only of the trams. Without quite realizing, I moved my hand up to the left temple and traced the outline of the hole in my head. After all these years the bone had fused but not solidified.

Chapter Twenty-Six

I sat in the old easy chair in the living room just before dinner, leafing through that morning's *New York Times*. I had been running behind all day since I was under pressure to finish a project at the publishing house where I worked. It caught my eye on the obituary page: "Mike Straus, prominent businessman, died a on golf course outside San Diego, Calif. He was 39 and succumbed to myocardial infarction." No. I slumped deeper into the battered chair, the paper crumpling in my lap. It can't be. The unwanted feelings started to seep in—the old times, the hurtful words.

I lifted the paper and continued.

"Mr. Straus took the family's modest business interests in Chicago and built them into a thriving conglomerate with holding companies, subsidiaries and interlocking family trusts. He accomplished this by absorbing failing companies and rebuilding them into giants in their fields. The companies he revitalized included the air carrier Eagle Air, which he salvaged from bankruptcy; Drive Away, the troubled car-rental company; and Motel 12, which he took from a local hostelry with three outlets into a nationwide chain. He also had major real estate holdings.

"'Mr. Straus was a respected player at the poker table of big business,' said Karen Ashbrook, analyst for Commonwealth Securities brokerage firm.

"Mr. Straus's brother, Edwin, gave this appraisal: 'Mike's tenacity and keen intuition enabled our family to salvage businesses that had been poorly handled and underappreciated. He turned them around, without massive layoffs or spin-offs of plants or equipment. Our success would not have been possible without Mike.'"

"He's dead," I told my wife, Barbara, who was working in the kitchen. Our young daughter Eve sat at the table reading a book, and our son Tom sprawled on the floor drawing on a pad. "Mike Straus."

"Your friend from Chicago?"

"Heart attack. Only 39. I never cleared it with him."

"What?"

"Something that came between us. Something that drove us apart."

"What's the matter, Daddy? You look so sad."

"I said a bad thing to a friend long ago. Now he's gone and it's too late."

"Oh, that is sad."

"Man, it never ends."

"I'm sorry, honey. I'm not following," Barbara said. "Your friend died too young. But that doesn't mean you're next."

"That's not what I'm talking about. I mean, the past never ends. You think you've come to terms, but it returns." Seeing her continued puzzlement, I raised my voice. "It has a life of its own. When I went back to Switzerland, I thought I had settled it. I believed I had. But now Mike dies, and wham! There it is."

"Don't, honey. It's over."

"Yeah, sure, it's over." I heard myself shouting.

As the children cringed at my volume, Barbara gave me a disapproving look and I retreated to the living room.

"Listen, Mike," I said aloud. "You'll always be my buddy. Damn!" I mashed the newspaper in a fist, threw it to the floor and walked to the window, blind to everything. "I'm sorry, Mike. So sorry."

I gazed at the darkness for many long moments. Then a basic urge to restore myself with my family took over. I returned to the kitchen, put an arm around Barbara and whispered an apology. I kissed the tops of the children's heads. I couldn't lose my three closest friends and allies.

"Story time," I called. "Daddy's gonna read you a story."

Eve ran into the living room with her book as she always did to claim a place on the best side of the chair. Tom followed, taking his time, to display his independence.

The warmth of their small bodies as they snuggled beside me exerted its own special healing. I began to read, and soon we were all transported by the tale. When the brave little child saved the dog and caught the crooks at the same time, we all had tears in our eyes. None more so than me.

Acknowledgments

This work was a long and at times painful project that has been alternately intriguing, teasing and agitating me for decades. During the course of its numerous drafts, many people have provided advice and inspiration.

I start with Mel Gussow, to whom the book is dedicated and without whose guidance, wisdom and editorial skills these pages would not exist. Another good friend, Jon Brand, also provided keen insights and intelligence.

Jeanne Stewart Chesanow lent a practiced professional hand, and Dr. Robert L. Chesanow provided vital medical information, as he has through the years. Dale Brown and Scott Burris were early readers and staked immensely useful guideposts. Other readers whose kind words gave me a boost include Anne Einhorn, Midge Ogletree, Gwinn Owens and Rhetta Barron. I would also like to acknowledge the inspiration of Sue Friedman, and other former classmates, with whom I had the joy of reconnecting in Chicago at a recent reunion.

O.B. Crowder deserves a large measure of gratitude for his trenchant suggestions while copyediting. Thanks to Sarah Lange for leading me expertly through the process of online publishing.

Deep appreciation goes to the National Endowment for the Arts and the John Simon Guggenheim Memorial Foundation for financial aid and encouragement when they were needed most.

Of course, any writing of mine must include heartfelt

recognition of the support and love given by my immediate family: my wife, Kathy Hughes von Hartz; my daughter, Maria von Hartz Shapiro; her husband, Jay Shapiro; their two wonderful children, Nicholas John and Katie Rose; my son, William von Hartz; and my sister Francesca Carr Coté.

No acknowledgment would be complete without words of devotion for my parents, Ernest von Hartz and Audrey Noonan von Hartz. They always backed me, believed in me and, indulged me. I am eternally grateful.

Made in the USA